USA TODAY BESTSELLING AUTHOR
SUSAN STRADIOTTO &
LEAH OMAR

High Heels & HEIFERS

Eden Prairie, MN

High Heels & Heifers

© 2023 Susan Stradiotto and Leah Omar

Published by:

Bronzewood Books

14920 Ironwood Ct.

Eden Prairie, MN 55346

Cover Design: Bronzewood Books

Interior Design: Bronzewood Books

Edited by: Enchanted Quill Press

Paperback ISBN-13: 978-1-949357-56-1

eBook ISBN-13: 978-1-949357-55-4

Publication history: A prior version of this book was published in the *My Funny Valentine* boxset in February 2023

For everyone who needs a little diversity
in their clean romance.

Love to you all!

Love is love,
Susan & Leah

Chapter One

I TAKE A DEEP BREATH, WIPE my sweaty palm on my pencil skirt, and steady my hand over the mouse pad on my MacBook Pro. The eighty-two-inch monitor at the end of the conference table churns as it works to refresh my presentation. This will be the first time my peers on the LivFit product development leadership team will see the video my marketing team put together. My heart thumps, loud in my ears and interrupting the thick silence in the fourteenth-floor executive conference room. My marketing team has done a knock-out job, but my mostly middle-aged male audience in this room will be a hard sell. Definitely more difficult to win over than my true target audience.

The screen finally refreshes to display a classy photo in black and white. The couple wears wedding attire, but their bodies are blurry in the background as they hold out their left hands toward the camera. Their fingers are the only part of the picture in focus, and the gold rings pop against the shades of gray. The woman's ring has a two-carat marquis diamond catching a ray of light and the man's version has three diamonds inlaid with a brushed gold band.

"That's stunning." Geoffrey Tanner, my boss and the VP of product development, reclines in his chair at the head of the table, holding a pen lengthwise between his fingers.

I smile and lift my brow. "Just wait." Then, I begin the video.

A montage of happy couples from every creed and persuasion moves across the screen. A man proposes, a woman slides a ring onto her partner's finger, a couple in wheelchairs roll down an aisle, two men in tuxedos dance. All of them wear the products my team has been working on for the last year. The narration has a James Earl Jones quality that truly highlights the two inaugural products for the new LivFit in Luxury line. When the video finishes, all the men in the room clap, some slower than others. Eddie, the newest team member and a fantastic hire in my opinion, seems the most enthusiastic. Bruce stifles a yawn as his hands meet only thrice.

Geoff tosses the pen on the table. "Nice work on the marketing side, Jack. How's the schedule and testing coming along?"

When I started at LivFit, Geoff was the first person to start calling me Jack. At first, it annoyed me, but then I liked the shortened version of Jacqueline. So much of our work is done via email, and having an androgynous name levels the playing field for me in this male dominated industry.

"Right on time." I flip to the next slide in my presentation and run down all the program statistics around cost, scope, schedule, and testing progress—all with a little green light beside them. I make sure to cover a couple of the issues the testing team found simply to demonstrate how the team is solving problems.

In the end, Geoff gives me a single, satisfied nod. "Eddie, how's the college-age project going?"

I stop sharing my screen and Eddie takes over, covering the other initiative that has recently started. LivFit's products have historically targeted the mid-thirties age market, where people are established and making enough money to afford wearable tech. My program aims to penetrate the jewelry market whereas Eddie's strategy is to win over the young adults. He claims the colleges he's visited to do market research all have a huge cycling population, so the latest concept is an anklet.

While he walks the team through the details of the proposal, I scan the room and the faces of my fellow directors. Aside from Eddie and myself, there's Bruce, the guy who should have retired ten years ago; then Derrick, Nathan, Sean, Calvin, and Anthony, each belonging to LivFit's original target market. As I watch them, I wonder why they give Eddie's presentation more energetic attention than they'd given mine. Doesn't matter. I'm going to hit the proverbial home run with this one. I can feel it in my bones.

"Thanks, Eddie." Apparently convinced, Geoff gives

him the go ahead and dismisses the meeting. "Have a good weekend everyone."

All the men get up and trickle toward the door. I stand to join them. It's Friday at 4 p.m., so I'm anxious to begin my working weekend. Saturday and Sunday are when I get in the most productivity, and that's necessary to be on my top game. I don't mind, though, because my goal is to take Geoff's position in another few years. And then . . . wouldn't CEO be nice?

Since I was sitting in the farthest chair from the exit, I'm the last in line to leave.

"Hey, Jack," my boss calls. "Can you hang back?"

I feel light in my high heels after that presentation and nearly bounce as I pivot around to face him. "Sure thing." In a few quick strides, I'm back where I started, placing my laptop and mobile phone on the table. I sit down and cross my legs. "What's up?"

Geoff scrolls through something on his laptop. "Our numbers for the last quarter are fabulous, and your market research is promising. The early ads for your rings have been getting a stellar response."

My spine straightens. I'm proud of the product my team has created. Being held after class to receive praise for a job well-done is something I thrive on. It was a weekly occurrence at Berkley. Although I'm preening, I try to remain humble. "You've let me build a wonderful product development team. And Marketing did all the imagery. Most of this early success is thanks to them."

He nods. "Keep this up and you'll be taking my job soon."

I strike a clutch-my-pearls pose. "Thank you." Then, my voice pitches teasingly. "But not unless you're planning to retire early." It might actually be right on time, but deference to superiors is always a good practice.

Geoff closes his computer and twists the ring on his left hand's third finger. "Are you doing anything fun this weekend?"

Odd that he held me back to ask about my plans. Surely, he's not going to—no. He and Eve are the happiest couple I could imagine. I flip a hand in his direction and shrug. "Oh, you know me. I'll probably hit the treadmill a couple of times, but aside from that, I have a lot of work to get through before Monday's quality review."

He chuckles. "You fit right in with this team, Jack. I'm so glad I fought to promote you."

"Me too, Geoff. This really is my dream job." I clutch my hand tighter around my laptop to avoid any of my nervous ticks. "And thank you again for that."

"No thanks necessary. You make me look great." He scoots forward in his chair and slides his laptop into his lap. "One more thing before we leave."

Mirroring his posture, I prompt, "Anything," and immediately regret the eagerness.

"The quarter's numbers and revised budget just came in, and I have some dollars to spend on a team-building event."

"That's wonderful. What are you thinking?"

"That's just the thing. I'm terrible with planning events. My wife handles everything social in my life." He pauses.

I feel suddenly heavy. Thoughts fire off left and right. The loudest is: *and so you thought that, because I'm the token skirt on the team, I would be eager to plan the team's social calendar?* I don't say it. In fact, I swallow the lump that's suddenly in my throat. Instead, I say, "You're lucky to have Eve to help you out with that," and force a smile.

"It's a decent budget." His eyes bore into me. "So, I thought you might like to handle the planning?"

Answer, Jack. You have to give him an answer. Quickly now.

Finally, I do. "I'll give it some thought over the weekend. If that's okay?"

He stands, glances at his watch, and then to the door. "Awesome. The budget is $3,000 per person. Just the leadership team and me. We'll need to do some team building or something too."

My stomach plummets. He's taken my answer as a yes, and there's not much I can do now to change that direction. I open my mouth to say something as Geoff starts walking toward the door.

Before disappearing from the conference room, he calls over his shoulder, "If you find something, go ahead and put it on the company card."

I slump back in the chair and pop upright again when his head pokes back inside.

"Oh, Jack?"

"Yeah?"

"Put some time on my calendar on Monday to chat

about what you decide."

Left alone in the fanciest of LivFit's conference rooms, I fight the urge to get up, pace around the room, and rant like a mad woman. How dare he? That's the most condescending, sexist point of view I've heard in a long time. I thought the diversity team was working to eradicate that kind of behavior but here I am. The only woman on an all-male team and assuming the position of Social Director. How stereotypical. I rarely even plan my own social calendar. My best friend, Mari, is the one dragging me all over San Francisco.

Speaking of Mari . . . I grab my phone off the desk and text: "Dartealing? I could use a strong tea about now."

THE CROWD AT DARTEALING LOUNGE two blocks from LivFit is already teeming, so I'm lucky to snag a small table with two Victorian-style chairs away from the majority of the crowd. Mari had a meeting that ran until five-thirty, so I order the first pot and wait alone for quite a while, watching the crowd. I finish my tea before my friend arrives and eat an orange slice from a plate of scones and fruits. The effects of the tea are warming my cheeks and easing my irritation over Geoff's request—a little, at least.

The waiter, a tall and skinny young man with a full-sleeve tattoo covering his left arm and black bangs that keep falling in his eyes, has checked on me a little too frequently and returns as soon as he sees my empty cup. He picks up the pot to pour some more. "The oranges are super sweet right now. Can I get you some more?"

"I think I should wait for my friend to arrive."

"A water?"

"That'd be great. Thanks!" I look down at my phone to see if Mari's texted. Nothing.

The waiter, who I think is leaving, doesn't. His voice sounds a bit husky when he starts to ask his next question but can't quite spit it out. "Is your friend a . . ."

He's cute. Nervous and awkward and probably six years my junior. I glance at his name tag and give him a sad smile. "Ah, Ryan." I hate this but dating him or anyone is not in my plans at the moment. Not to mention how limited his experience likely is. After the string of college boyfriends who usually headbutted me before they found my lips to kiss, I'm just not into guys. Maybe that'll change someday, or maybe I'll find someone whose kisses sweep me off my feet. I'm only twenty-eight. So, I have plenty of time. "My friend is—"

"—is here." Mari dashes around the waiter, saving me from the awkward situation.

Ryan straightens. "Oh. In that case, can I bring you another round of tea?" When I nod, he asks my friend, "A cup for you?"

"Totally. Bring me what she's having." When Ryan starts to leave, she calls after him. "Hey, honey. I'm famished. I'm ready to order food too." She glances at me. Sparkles light her bright blue eyes. "You ready?"

I nod as she opens the menu and order. "I'll take the smoked salmon sandwich."

Mari closes the menu and hands it to Ryan. "Bring

me the roast beef and blue sandwich." When he leaves, she drapes her napkin in her lap, leans on her elbow on the arm of the chair, and lets out a loud sigh.

I grimace at her order. "How in the world do you put beef and blue cheese in your mouth?"

She sweeps her blonde hair over one shoulder with an eye roll. "I'm a carnivore, love. Not everyone swears off meat like you."

"I eat meat."

She stares me down.

"What? It's true." I finish the last of my tea and set the cup in the saucer. It jitters a little, but I'm relishing all the caffeine at the moment. "I'm a pescatarian. It's heart healthy."

She eyes my shaky hand accusingly as I lower the cup to the table. "Jacqueline, haven't we had this conversation already?"

I gasp. "Really Mari?" How dare she? She knows I've gone by Jack since my sophomore year of high school. About the same time I decided to stop eating land animals. My doctor-parents most often served fish at home, except for the occasional tamales Nana made with chicken. That's my one exception.

She gives me the "I'm over the diet talk" look, and I relent.

"Fine, but don't call me Jacqueline. It makes me feel like a little old lady with blue hair and a mailbox shaped purse."

Ryan brings our drinks and two glasses of ice water.

We both take a drink.

Mari sighs after her first sip and pins me with her gaze. "Fine. *Jack*. What's got you in a tizzy today? I'm usually the one calling you to go out on the town. And judging by that shake, you've had a full pot of this tea all on your own. Which one is it, anyway?"

Scratching my jaw just below my ear, I make a face. Mari knows me too well and that I'm usually more reserved, not willing to keep myself up with caffeine on Friday nights when I usually get most of my office work done early Saturday mornings.

"Out with it," she demands.

"I have to plan a team-building event for all the *male* directors on Geoff's product development team."

Mari fishes the orange out of her glass and takes a bite. "And? What's the problem?"

She's always been the more risqué one of us and I saved her more than once from a drunken night in college. She's definitely not one to be concerned with equality issues, and sometimes I envy her ability to be so aloof about it all. But then again, she works at a female owned startup company doing independent product testing and reviews. She doesn't experience the same types of discrimination as I do at the old-boys club where I work.

"It's insulting. Just because I have curves, Geoff assumes I am excited to do the girly thing and plan a big party."

"Big?"

"Yeah. He gave me a budget of three thousand a

head."

Mari's jaw drops.

"Tell me about it. Insane, right? But whatever I decide, I'm stuck with eight men, most of whom don't value what I bring to the business table."

Mari sits back, looking at me as if what I'm saying is an issue with my overactive imagination. "Don't you get more attention being the only girl?"

"It's not about attention, Mari." I wish it was easier to explain that success, or lack thereof, because of my sex is insulting. "Maybe I should start wearing pants suits. The kind with a sports coat and tie. I mean, I already go by Jack and have short hair. It'd basically be switching out my wardrobe and forgoing the makeup." I shiver at the last part. Even though I want them to treat me equally, I have no desire to forsake makeup and adorable shoes. I like my pencil skirts, heels, and a good spa day from time to time.

"Back the truck up a bit." Mari shakes her head and waves a hand in the air. "You get to spend three-thousand dollars on something fun for the team? And you're complaining?"

I raise my brows and nod.

"Geez, we can't spend ten dollars per person on lunch for the team at my work." Mari puts aside an orange peel and takes another sip. When she finishes, a devilish blue light flashes in her eyes. "Maybe . . ."

Shoot! I know that shift. That slide into her famous "I have a brilliant idea" look on her face. "What are you cooking up?"

Mari leans closer to me. "Just hear me out, 'kay?"

This is scary, but she usually does have imaginative ideas. Crass sometimes but creative nonetheless.

"I saw this thing come across our potential project list at work. A vacation. It's all-inclusive and runs about twenty-five hundred a head, if I remember correctly."

"I'm listening." I eye her sideways. An all-inclusive vacation sounds fantastic. Spa, beach, sand. Heaven. So, there's gotta be a catch.

"It's in New Mexico. Hang on." She grabs her phone. "I'm sure I can find it."

My brow furrows. "New Mexico? There isn't anything in New Mexico except tumbleweeds and abandoned roads. Has to be Mexico, right?"

Mari grins and turns her phone to face me. On the screen, there are . . . cows.

I narrow my eyes and read: *Thoroughgood Ranch Cattle Drives.* "Seriously? No way. No cows."

"Just hear me out. You said they expect you to be the girly one. This is anything but. Yeah?" She bobs her head slowly.

I hate to admit it, but she's not wrong. So, eventually, my lips curl into a smile and I answer, "Sure, but—"

Mari's hand pops up to stop my objection "And your team is strictly the suit-and-tie type, right?"

I'm starting to see the promise in her idea. I don't think I've seen one of my peers in anything but designer clothes. Sure, like me, they work out regularly, so we're all in decent enough shape for this. I mean, we do work for a healthy lifestyle company, but this would definitely throw them all off their games. However, it also means I would have to deal with cows. And horses. And dirt. I start shaking my head again.

"C'mon, Jack." Mari widens her eyes. "We're from a small town. There were farms nearby. You even had some ranch down the road, right?"

"A Buddhist retreat, Mari. There weren't any horses or cows on that 'ranch.'"

"Bah." She rolls her eyes. "You can handle this. No problem. But . . . can your coworkers?"

I chew the inside of my lip and think about Bruce. He had hip replacement surgery earlier this year and is getting around better than he did before the surgery. Although, how keen will he be to ride a horse? Perhaps suggesting this will show that I'm not capable of being Geoff's social director. That alone would make the trip worth the trouble.

I keep noodling on the team and their probable reaction as our dinner arrives. My boss and the quartet of thirty-somethings . . . well, their hobby is golf. Regardless, their preferred sport likely means they are not fit for something like ranching or cattle drives either. Eddie, now, he is as flexible as a rubber band and eager to boot. He'll love the idea. That's good, because the others love him. He'll sell it for me.

"I did go to a horse camp once when I was eight," I muse.

Mari watches me, lips pursed, eyes narrowed and her head nods.

Then, I recall something else, gasp, and reach for my purse.

"What?" my friend asks.

Biting my lip, I glance at her as I retrieve my LivFit MasterCard. "Geoff already gave me the go-ahead to book something."

Mari snatches the card out of my hand and lifts her glass. "Nine of you, right?"

"Yep." I toast. "This is an awful idea. But, also, brill."

Chapter Two

Luca

ASPER LOOKS AT ME WITH his big brown eyes, and like I always do, I give in and offer him one more carrot. He rubs his long head against my shoulder, his favorite way to say thank you, and I finish brushing his deep brown coat until it shines. It's not fair for me to have my favorites, but Jasper is my boy, and I've told him more about myself than I've shared with anyone else. Horses are magical creatures. No judgment. They accept people for who they are. And, usually, Jasper can sense what I'm thinking or when I feel down, and he doles out love unconditionally.

"Alright, boy, it's time for you to get some sleep. You had a busy day."

I close the door to Jasper's stable and rub the one small white spot between his eyes. "I'll be back bright and early."

All the horses start settling in, and I do a check to make sure their stalls are secure for the night. I glance back into the barn one last time before I shut the outer door and walk toward the main house.

The house is quiet, and there are no signs of Wyatt and Emma. I walk into the kitchen, grab myself a Coke from the fridge, and hold the cold bottle against my forehead. After a few seconds, I open it on the edge of the counter and put it against my lips. I look around the rustic cabin and can't believe it's been two years since I left my old world to join my best friend Wyatt and his wife here on their ranch. It's changed so much since I've arrived, and with the breaking of land a couple of miles down the road. By this time next year, I'll have my own home on this five-thousand-acre ranch on the eastern edge of the Santa Fe National Forest. The location has a million and a half acres of the most beautiful undiscovered scenery this world has to offer.

Before settling into the ranch office, I grab another Coke from the fridge, and then I fire up the laptop. Business has been steady for the past few months, and when I click on the reservation page, there's a new one waiting our attention. The reservation is for nine people from LivFit, a health technology company out of San Francisco. I hold my drink to my mouth and let it pour in.

"What's the good word, Luca?"

I swivel my chair to look at my best friend, Wyatt, who stands in the doorway.

"Business has been good," I say. "Can we refuse a

reservation?"

Wyatt laughs off my question, but I already know the answer. These things are half of our livelihood here on the ranch.

He grabs a chair at the desk next to mine. "Looks like a high-maintenance group?"

I study the screen. "A corporate retreat. Product Developers out of San Francisco. I can picture it now. Maybe we can get 'em on a technicality like one of them exceeding the weight limit for our horses."

It's a last-ditch effort to get out of hobnobbing with a group of corporate managers for a week, and I know it.

Wyatt leans in, takes my laptop, and swivels it in his direction. "What are you talking about? This group looks great. Nine people. Looks to be all men. Five nights, six days, and they bought our most expensive package. Seems like a winning reservation to me."

"City slickers." I scoff. "You've never worked in Corporate America. These guys aren't going to know a saddle horn from a doorknob. That's the kind of people about to show up on our doorstep."

"If anyone has the patience for city slickers, it's you, buddy." Wyatt taps me on the shoulder. "You spent a decade in that environment. You know how to talk golf and stocks, and you'll have these guys charmed on day one." Before he leaves the office, he mumbles, "Plus, they work for a fitness company. How out of shape can they be? We may not even need Emma to tag along on this ride."

I've known Wyatt since we were matched as

roommates in Stern Hall at Stanford. He was there to study business management, already knowing that he would move back to New Mexico after college and take over his parents' ranch that had been in his family for over a hundred years. I didn't know what I wanted to study when I first started at Stanford. All I knew is that I wanted to be a Vice President at a *Fortune* 500 corporation. We both reached our goals, yet here we both are, at the ranch.

"What can I help with?" Emma walks in and takes the seat that Wyatt vacated.

"Room assignments, I suppose. I'll print out all the paperwork."

Emma studies the list of the nine men coming to stay with us in three days. We always make sure there is time between retreats to let the horses rest, to recuperate ourselves, and then a full day to pack for being on the road for nearly six days. It's a lot of work, but I've never been more satisfied at the end of each day than I am on this ranch.

"I can't wait for the day when you'll have your own house and our bunkhouse is built for visitors. Then, Wyatt and I can finally make this house our own without welcoming people into it every other week." Emma sighs and leans back in her chair.

Their house is massive, but it doesn't feel like it is when the first night of all retreats is spent here before we go out on the trails and sleep in tents underneath the stars. There are five decent sized bedrooms, and then a loft, so even though it isn't the most convenient, we have the space.

But I get how it would be an inconvenience to Wyatt and Emma who so frequently open their house to random strangers from everywhere in the country. Wyatt shared that they are talking about starting a family. Things will change significantly for us when that happens.

"Sorry to break it to you, Luca, but you're going to have to bunk up with someone on night one. It's the only way everyone will have a warm bed to land on."

"I figured that much."

It's not unusual that I have to share my bedroom for these larger retreats, which is another reason I can't wait until my house is complete. I bring in an air mattress, throw it in the corner, and it's the best night of sleep the retreat attendee will get, because it's on the ground from the first day onward.

"Here." Emma hands me the paper that just printed. "Here are room assignments. And everyone can suck it up, because it's a team-building event, and I refuse to take room requests."

I look through the stack that Emma handed me.

"And voila. I just filed all of their medical information and waivers." Emma smiles as she does a final click on her computer before closing it.

"This place couldn't run without you, Emma," I say, leaning back in my chair and resting my head against my arms.

"No truer words, Luca. No truer words." Emma organizes the pile of papers on the desk and ruffles my hair before she leaves the office.

Jack

I'm scanning through emails on my phone, waiting for the luggage to drop. My team members' status reports are rolling in, and I need to make sure the project is on track before I hop on the back of a horse and commune with nature for a week. My contacts blur a little and I blink several times against the dry air, which was the first thing I noticed when we stepped off the plane at Albuquerque's airport. The arid climate also sucked all the moisture from my skin, so I hope there is lotion easily accessible in my bag. Having lived near the coast for my entire life, my skin is accustomed to constant humidity.

Eddie saunters over, pulling his carry-on. "The others are heading out to meet the van. You okay? Your eyes look a bit red."

I smile and drop my phone to my side, swinging it idly by the rhinestone ring on the back. "They're just adjusting. Contacts don't do so well with sudden humidity changes. No worries though; I've got drops in my suitcase."

Beyond Eddie, my boss leads the way outside, and the other directors on my team cut me annoyed glances before following. It's still hard for me to believe no one else checked a bag. Where could they possibly be hiding the gear they would need for this excursion?

Eddie gives a quite dramatic eye roll and slumps his weight into one hip. "So, while we're waiting, why don't you . . . *spill the beans* . . . on how you came up with this whole trip. Oh, wait, hold that thought." He smirks. "*My eyeballs are floating.* I'll be right back." He shoves a book he was holding into my hands and dashes toward the men's room.

There are three dozen tabs marking the pages. I flip it over to read the cover—*1001 Purely Southern Sayings.* When I flip to the first tab, both the sayings he just laid on me are highlighted. I shake my head. This ought to be rich.

A few minutes later, Eddie comes jogging back in my direction and he holds his hands out for the book.

"I'm not sure I should give this back," I say, quirking one eyebrow.

He snatches it out of my hand playfully. "*Well, I declare.* You need to *quit being ugly,* girl."

"How many have you memorized?"

Eddie gives me a coy look. "*I reckon* you'd like to know?" His false southern accent is horrendous. "Anyway, you were just about to tell me about how you came up with this crazy idea of yours."

I open my mouth to speak, but he grasps onto my arm with a wide-eyed expression, as if he's worried he somehow offended me. He leans in and lowers his voice. "I mean, it's going to be a riot for sure. I can't imagine most of this team on horseback. I, for one, am excited about the sport of it all."

"It'll be different. That's for sure." In truth, it came as a surprise that everyone went along with the idea so easily. Perhaps—no probably—the reason was because Geoffrey made the announcement rather than me.

A red siren light beams on top of the carousel as

a buzzing fills the air, and the whirring mechanical sound announces the bags are about to arrive. The people waiting herd forward.

Eddie holds out a hand. "You joining in?"

With a chuckle, I answer, "Nah. I'll wait till mine drops and then move in." Fortunately, it falls within the first dozen bags. I worked from the airport this morning, and checking in early obviously paid off. First bags checked equal last ones on the plane and, therefore, are the first to drop. At least I'll be quick to join the others. I pull my Gucci laptop bag higher on my shoulder and start to move.

Eddie grabs my elbow. "Watch my bag, and I'll get it. The pink one with leopard print, right?"

I nod.

When he grabs it from the belt and returns, he pats it twice. "You're going to make quite the statement at the ranch with this thing. Why's it so heavy?"

"Didn't you read the brochure about all the things you need? Light weight clothes, layers, jacket, sunscreen, toiletries . . . Boots—those things are huge and heavy! And there's no way I'm making it through an entire week with only one pair of shoes."

Eddie lifts one brow and scans down my outfit, finishing with his eyes on my high heels. "Everyone else just wore their boots. You're not going to have room to bring multiple pairs."

I reach for the handle on the rolling hard-sided suitcase. "I'll find a way. They'll just have to understand . . . I only travel in style."

"I don't think you do anything *not* in style." He chuckles.

The clock on the wall above the doors says the van should have been here ten minutes ago. "We should go."

The sidewalk outside is cracked and heaving, and my suitcase lurches and falls to the side. Eddie leans toward me to help, but I wave him off. I work out regularly for this kind of occasion. "I've got it." The suitcase is big and awkward for me to lift, but I manage.

At the van, Eddie hops inside and moves to the back. A man wearing a cowboy hat, jeans, and a belt buckle the size of a salad plate takes my suitcase and tosses it into the back as if it were filled with air.

"Thanks," I say when the driver returns.

"You're Jacqueline?" He offers me a hand to assist me into the van.

My colleagues are all waiting. Most browse their mobiles, but Bruce sits in the passenger seat, staring out the window.

"Jack," I correct the driver and, with a glance at his hand, I turn away. This was my plan, and I can do it for myself. As soon as my foot lands on the uneven cement off the curb, my heel wrenches in a crack and I stumble forward. My cheeks flare with heat, and I peek up through my lashes to see if the driver saw my clumsiness.

I'm not in luck, though. He smirks, issues a stifled laugh, and grabs my elbow. I recover quickly and he supports my weight as I clamber into the van.

"Thank you," I mumble after my hind-end hits the

bench seat next to my boss.

"Ma'am." He tips his head and places my laptop bag next to me.

Geoffrey naturally asks the apparent question of the day. "You okay?"

"Fine." I slip off the shoe and stare at the broken heel. It would have been fine, except these are my favorite and most comfortable Jimmy Choo pumps.

The driver slides inside and holds out his hand over his shoulder. "Let me see them. You won't make it three steps at the ranch in those, even if one wasn't broken."

I slide off the other shoe and hand both over. He pulls a huge knife off the dash, unsheathes it, and slices the little strip of leather still tethering the heel. I bite my lip as this travesty unfolds before me. Next, he wedges the tip of the vicious-looking blade into the seam on the good shoe. With a snap and to my great horror, the other shoe is heel-less too.

Blow it off, I tell myself and accept the now-flats. I never, ever wear flats. Getting there and into my room can't come soon enough. There's a pair of Athleta leggings and tennis shoes calling my name. Maybe I can get in a run before the happy hour orientation.

"Hope you've got something in that crate you brought better than those," the driver says and drops the van into gear. "Get comfy, everyone. We've got an hour on the road."

After turning on my hot spot, I pull out my laptop and settle in for the ride. The team is silent except for someone who starts snoring in the back. Country music twangs over the radio, and I do my best to block it out and focus on the latest testing statistics the team sent over. Everything appears on track, so I send out a "great work, team" email and close the computer just as we pull off the pavement onto a dirt road. There's a sign on the side of the dirt path: *Welcome to the wild west. Thoroughgood Ranch: 10 miles.*

The van bounces, and I look for something to hold on to. There's nothing but the backs of the seats in front of me. I reach forward, when the front right tire dips into a huge rut. My laptop goes flying onto the floor between the driver and passenger seats, and the only thing that keeps me from sliding onto the floor myself is Geoffrey's arm extending across my chest.

He arches one brow. "Maybe you should buckle up."

Luca

RETREAT DAY CAME TOO QUICKLY, and I feel like I haven't sat down in over twenty-four hours from all the preparation. Wyatt, Emma, and I huddle, and look over our final plans, knowing that a van full of LivFit's finest will be arriving at our doorstep.

"Let's let everyone get settled in their rooms, and then we'll have happy hour where we can go through expectations before having dinner," Wyatt says.

"It looks like Jack is the organizer for Liv Fit, so let's sit down with him as well so he can let us know everything we should be aware of with their group," I say to nodding heads.

"Are you sure you want to take Jasper out on his

inaugural retreat?"

"He's ready, Emma," I say. "He's been working so hard, and his temperament is getting better. He deserves to be out there with his buddies."

"I think you're right," Wyatt says.

"They should be here any minute, so I'm going to tend to the horses, do a double check on equipment, and meet you all inside in no time at all."

As I walk to the barn, a dark van with tinted windows comes into view as it goes underneath our sign welcoming them to Thoroughgood Ranch. Wyatt and Emma tell me that I come off as a curmudgeon, and maybe I do, but the excitement I have when a group shows up is unparalleled. The first time I visited this ranch was when Wyatt brought me home for Spring Break our freshman year of college. I fell in love with it at first sight, and my hope is that everyone else loves it as much as I do.

I do horseshoe checks on the twelve horses that will accompany us on this cattle drive, and then I make sure we have enough food packed for them for our five-night trip.

"It's going to be an adventure," I say to no horse in particular. "We're going to make these city folk fall in love with our open-air office, do you hear me?"

There is a lot of gear packed for this trip, and hopefully all the attendees realize that they're the ones who have to haul a lot of it. Everyone will sleep in a single tent they'll need to pitch. There's food, tools, horse gear. As I look at everything placed in neat piles, it looks like we'll be away for five months, not five nights.

As I walk inside, I hear voices ringing out from the great room, but instead of checking on the group, I decide to retreat to my room in hopes of getting in a quick shower before I join everyone for happy hour.

I turn the doorknob, but it's locked, so I grab my key from the front pocket of my jeans. During non-retreat times, this is my private bedroom with a spacious en suite. But when we're hosting a retreat, I'm room number five. All the way down the hallway, last door on the left.

"What are you doing in here?"

My heartbeat nearly escapes my chest as I look across the room at a woman who was starting to unzip her skirt just as I walked in. Her mouth hangs open, her lips a beautiful shade of red to match her blushing complexion. Her dark hair is tucked behind her ears. And the sound that comes out of my mouth surprises us both.

I . . . laugh.

"Who are you?" she asks again. "Geoff threw me a key for room number five. Said that's where I was assigned. I assumed I had a private room."

Her voice sounds shrill, and I look at her suitcase—pink, leopard print. Figures. Her clothes are strewn across my bed. All of her belongings. On *my* bed. And I wonder: what did she *not* bring?

"I'm so sorry, ma'am," I say, trying to compose myself. "There must be a misunderstanding. This is my bedroom."

As if she doesn't believe me, she puts her heels back on her feet, marches over to me, and shows me the wood carved horse attached to a key with the number five on it.

"Five. I'm in room number five."

"Ma'am, again, I'm sorry for the mix up. I work here too, and we were expecting an all-male group, so someone has accidentally put you into a room with me."

"I won't room with you," she says, planting a fist on her hip. Her shoulders are rigid as if she's trying so hard to take up more space than her little frame will allow. This little lady obviously has a lot to prove, but in truth, she's not a very large woman.

"No, of course not," I say. "I'll talk to Emma, and because we are out of beds, I'll make arrangements for you to bunk with her tonight, and Wyatt can bunk with me. My bedding is clean. I'd be happy if you took my bed."

"That's the least you can do," she says but then her voice takes on a slightly less sharp tone. Maybe she is aware of how shrewish she sounded with that remark. She shoots out a hand, making me blink. "I'm Jacqueline. People call me Jack."

"Luca. Ah, people call me . . . Luca." I take her delicate, soft hand in mine, so at contrast with how sharply she thrust it forward.

Her face contorts before she pulls her hand away and wipes it on her skirt. I scan my palm to make sure there's no dirt lingering from re-shoeing the horses earlier. I washed them when I came in, but there's always the possibility.

Seeing nothing from the stables, I say, "I did wash up when I came in."

She runs her hands over her ear as if she's tucking her

hair back, but it's already there. Nervous tick, perhaps? Her lips pucker, hidden thoughts flitting behind her eyes. Then, she says, "Well, Luca, I'd love to get changed before our orientation at happy hour, if you don't mind."

Jack nods toward the door, and her sharp tone is back. I care about my life too much to ask permission to use my shower so I can change before our gathering, but I do need a change of clothes.

"Of course," I say and reach for the top drawer on my dresser. "As soon as I grab a change of clothes." I keep talking as I pull out a pair of jeans and clean button-down shirt. "I'll talk to Emma, and we'll do the switcheroo. Sorry again for the inconvenience."

I duck out through the still open door, and it slams behind me. The lock clicks from the other side. So, that was Jack, the corporate retreat organizer, and most definitely not a man. No. She's a woman, with very soft hands, huge brown eyes, and more sass than might exist in the whole of New Mexico.

I'm still laughing when I run into Emma in the hallway, carrying a few bottles of water in her hand. "What's so funny?" she asks.

I point with my thumb down the hall, toward my bedroom. "We'll need to reconfigure the rooms, Emma. I just met my supposed-to-be-roommate Jack."

"Yeah?" Emma says. "And?"

"And," I snicker. "Jack is a woman."

"Oh," Emma's face drops. "A woman? What? Are you sure?"

"Emma," I touch her shoulder, "I know a woman when I see one, and she is most certainly female. So, I will be joining Wyatt in your room tonight, and you will be on an air mattress in my room because Jack has already claimed the bed."

"Well, this retreat just got interesting, didn't it?"

"You have no idea," I respond. But leave out the part where I walked in on Jack about to undress. I'll save that story for another day.

Chapter Three

Jack

ICAN'T BELIEVE THE NERVE OF that man just walking into my room like that. At least he's gone now, but he had the indecency to laugh at my indelicate situation. I lean my back on the door I locked behind him and pause. The sad thing about the situation is . . . I didn't mind having his eyes on me, and that's a first.

A shiver runs over my body, and the hairs on my arms stand on end. Luca. His name is as exotic as the jungle green in his eyes. Then, there's the drawl in his "ma'am." Just mmm. *Stop it, Jack!* I go back to the far side of the bed to finish changing clothes. When I release it, my still unzipped pencil skirt falls to the floor and I fish out my workout gear. My brand new Athleta leggings feel fabulous hugging my calves and thighs. Once they're on, I pull on a wicking T-shirt and sit down on the bed to tie my Brooks runners before hanging up my dress clothes. Driving from the airport to this place took far longer than I'd anticipated, so I won't get a chance to run before we gather before dinner. I'll make sure to eat light so I can get the workout in afterward.

A cup of good tea is off the table for now. But maybe there will be some left when I get back. A soak in the tub with a robust Cabernet sounds delightful.

On the bed, my phone lights up and shows the time. "Sugar honey iced tea!" I blurt and rush to the door. I'm about to be late for my own party. Before I leave, I turn around and scan the room. It's neat, except for my suitcase. I'll have to clean up my clothes later, but Luca shouldn't mind. Heck, he shouldn't even be back here until after I'm gone, but I still had to bunk with someone named Emma.

Okay, time to go. I grab my laptop and the stack of more waivers from the LivFit lawyers and reach for the knob. My eyes fall to a candle on the dresser, which is the only decoration or knick-knack around. Everything else is super tidy. I can appreciate that as someone who believes everything should have its place. With a smile, I open the door.

As soon as I exit, I run smack dab into somebody—a woman, who's half a head taller than me—and drop my laptop along with all the papers on the floor. We both bend down to grab the mess, and it occurs to me that she must be the one who will be rooming with me in Luca's place. When I look up, the top of my head smashes into her nose.

"Oweee!" Her hand covers the bridge of her nose and both eyes.

I sputter. "Oh, geez. I'm so, so sorry!" I say, reaching

for her hands.

But she pushes away my hand. "It's okay. I'll be okay." She stretches her mouth into a long o-shape to move her nose and removes her hand from the bridge of her nose. Her eyes water, but it doesn't seem like her nose will bruise. Thank goodness.

"Emma?" I ask. My hands still fumble with my mess, but I keep one eye on her.

She sniffles and wipes away her tears but she answers, "That's me. You must be Jack?"

"That's me. I'm usually not this clumsy." I feel my face heating for the second, no the third, time today, if you count the heel incident. No one is going to see me as a leader me if I keep having these incidents. "I can't tell you how sorry I am. I have a little medical experience. Do you want me to look at it?"

"No. No. It's really okay." She flashes me a still-watery-eyed smile. "This place can throw people from the city off kilter. My husband and I run the ranch. I should apologize to you about the room mix-up. We're kind of tight on rooms for a group or size, so we have everybody bunking up. We just assumed Jack was a guy and wouldn't mind sleeping in the same room with our friend Luca. He's building the house you might have seen in the distance, but he's living here at the moment."

I stand, my laptop and papers tucked back in the crook of my arm, and offer her my hand for a shake. I don't mind in the slightest that she took me for a guy. That's why I chose the name Jack. "No worries," I tell her. "Happens all the time."

She shoves her hands in the front pockets of her jeans and tips her head down the hall. Her long French braid sways a little with the motion. "Why don't I show you to our dining room?"

As we walk, I remember my presentation. "Do you have a projector? I have a deck I'd like to share with the team before we get into the orientation, assuming my computer works after I've dropped it twice today."

Emma chuckles. "We don't do much here in the way of computers or presentations."

I purse my lips. "I suppose I could just do a quick virtual meeting and everyone could follow along on their own computers."

"That requires a strong internet signal, right?"

"Any high speed should do."

"Well, ours is sketchy at best, and it's worse at night. Besides, I didn't see any of your colleagues with computers when they were gathering in the dining room." Emma turns the corner and starts descending the stairs.

I slow and my mouth gapes. Really? They don't have a reliable internet connection? What exactly have I gotten myself into? Thinking I could fire up my hotspot, I check my phone's signal. One bar. I sigh and follow Emma the rest of the way to the dining room.

When I walk in, I see how right she was. All eight of my male counterparts stand around with various flavors of soda, in hand. Most wear jeans, boots, and a T-shirt. Eddie's already wearing his brand-spanking-new cowboy hat.

I narrow my eyes at him. "Don't you think that could have waited for tomorrow?"

"Just thought *I'd get all gussied up.*" He winks and tips back his Coke.

I scowl, but looking around, no one seems to be in the mood for anything professional. It sucks to be the stickler in the group. However, HR impressed on me that I had to go through the waivers and make sure every last person signed before they threw one leg over a saddle. I drop my laptop and papers on the end of the table just as two cowboys come strutting in the room.

One is wearing a cowboy hat too but sheds it as he enters. I clear my throat and nudge Eddie, who gets the drift and removes his hat too. The cowboy's face is round and dimpled, and I like him instantly. He must be Wyatt, the person on the emails. The taller one is Luca, and he's carrying a stack of papers too. Probably the ones we all signed before.

"Before everyone gets a little tipsy, I need ya'll to gather around for a briefing," Luca says.

What's he doing? My mouth hangs for a couple of breaths before I recover. He's stealing my thunder. "Luca?"

His eyes lift to meet mine, one dark brow arched in question, and I forget what I was about to say.

Then, suddenly, I shake myself out of it. "I need to get some business out of the way before we dive into the ranch's orientation." Jutting a hip, I wait while he stands straighter, a little surprised, apparently. "If you don't mind, that is."

Luca

My eyes follow the brunette's hip as it juts out, paper in her hand, her index finger tapping against them.

"Sorry, ma'm. It looks like I'll be co-presenting with you this fine evening."

She wrinkles up her forehead, puckers her lips, and then concedes. I stand taller, fighting a smile, when she rolls her eyes. I can't quite figure out why I find her better-than-everyone attitude a bit . . . cute. It should be the most annoying thing ever.

"Okay, LivFit. Eyes on me," Jack says.

The conversations in the room come to a halt, and Jack has the attention of the entire room. I can't tell by people's looks if it's respect or fear that I see. I'm positioned directly behind her and try to divert my eyes from her shape in those overly priced leggings.

"Thoroughgood Ranch should have your waivers for their legal needs. But you also need to sign these from LivFit. HR insisted." She puts the stack on the table and continues talking. "Read it carefully, but it basically says you are taking this risk on your own accord, and if something goes wrong, you won't sue the company, etcetera, etcetera."

"And these," I point to the waivers that Emma hands me, "are the waivers that say you also won't sue Thoroughgood."

Jack starts picking up the forms her team has signed and hands them to me.

"The entire purpose of a corporate retreat," Jack starts

to say as I take a few steps back to where Wyatt stands. If there is something I can't hear one more time in this lifetime, it's the purpose of forced corporate bonding. I've taken part and planned too many to realize they are a joke and nothing more than a boondoggle for bored employees to stick around for a little longer.

I look at the LivFit employees sitting around the table. In each group we have out here there are similarities. There is the take charge person. That's obviously Jack, but I haven't quite picked out the others on my list yet. There's always someone who was forced to come and would like to be anywhere else. There is the boss, who probably shouldn't be. There is the person up for anything—that seems to be the younger kid on the end. And there is always the person that thinks they know more about ranching than the actual ranchers do. I wonder which one that will be.

Wyatt leans in and whispers into my ear. "Jack being a woman was sure a surprise."

"You're telling me." The neck of my shirt suddenly feels too tight, so I pull at the collar.

"I'm sure her mind is brilliant, but Emma and I may have both agreed that we think she's pretty hot too."

I chuckle, which causes Jack to glance back and roll her eyes before continuing her corporate diatribe.

"Oh, she's hot alright," I say. "She probably also wears lotion that costs more than my yearly supply of shampoo, and her single pair of leggings costs more than my entire wardrobe."

Again, with the leggings. I need to stop thinking

about those darn things. "Wyatt, I'm sure she's a nice enough gal. But me leaving California was leaving superficial women like her behind. Trust me when I say they are all the same."

Wyatt punches me in my arm. "You sound a bit judgy there, Luca. Remember how much money we are making on this LivFit retreat."

"Yeah, yeah," I concede. Jack's big brown eyes turn to me. Again.

"You're up, cowboy," she says.

Jack takes a few steps backward, and our shoulders graze each other as I step forward.

"Okay, LivFit." I choose *her* words and she huffs at me. Perfect. I squelch a satisfied smile and continue. "The next few days aren't for the faint of heart. This is a real cattle drive. We're not out on this ranch pretending to be cowboys."

A cough echoes out from behind me, and I turn to see Jack, not so subtly correcting me.

"Or cowgirls," I add. "We will be actual cattle herders. We'll sleep under the stars; we'll work harder than anyone has ever worked, and we'll get our cattle safely to the next spot on their journey."

Wyatt takes a step beside me. "You're going to see your colleagues laugh and most definitely cry. You're going to get dirty, stink real bad, and also have the best week of your life. This, my friends, is corporate bonding at its finest."

Wyatt turns to wink at me. He's a bit naïve about

that rat race and easily buys into the corporate bonding talk. If he only knew how much malarkey went into posturing for rank in that narcissistic environment.

Jack ducks out from behind me, her brows peaked. "We'll still be able to shower this week, right?" She looks so innocent I can't help but laugh.

"If you want to skinny dip in a stream with the leeches, you can take all the baths you want this week, ma'am."

The mortified look on her face is going to keep me going the next few days.

Jack

EMMA BRINGS IN A HUGE cast iron pot and sets it at the center of the table. My colleagues sit straighter in their chairs and reach for their napkins. I can almost see their mouths watering by the collective motions. Wyatt and Emma sit side-by-side on the far side of the table, and the only two chairs remaining open are facing each other at the end near the window. Luca slides into the one opposite of me.

My stomach rumbles, and I remember I haven't eaten since breakfast. The scent is rich, garlic and oniony goodness. "What's for dinner? It smells amazing."

Emma smiles toward the cowboy beside her and takes his hand under the table. "It's Wyatt's mother's recipe. We call it Rancher's Hash." My eyes drift down to her left hand and the princess-cut rock sitting there. Then, I try to see Wyatt's hand, but his is out of sight.

Wyatt tips his head forward in a single nod. "I shot the elk that's in there last fall. One of the biggest ones I've bagged."

Across from me, Luca points the fork in his jewelry-free left hand toward Wyatt. "I remember that one. It took both of us to pull that twelve-point buck into the Ranger." He reaches for the breadbasket sitting nearby. "Good call, Emma, on dinner. Best to get the group started off with the food we'll be eating for the next week."

As Luca pulls out a piece of cornbread and bites into it, the image of men with rifles and blood pouring out of a poor animal runs through my mind, and I go suddenly cold. I thought I'd submitted my dietary restrictions along with the registration information, but apparently, I either didn't or they forgot.

Luca leans forward slightly, readying to stand. "Jack? You feel okay?" He's poised as if he's about to jump up from his seat and run my way.

Sucking in a breath, I blink my eyes several times. "Yeah. I'm fine." I look over to Emma, who is sinking a serving spoon into the brownish stew-like stuff in the pot. "I don't mean to be disrespectful, but do you have anything like fish? A good salmon, perhaps? Or something vegetarian? I'd be happy to cook."

Across the table, Luca raises both brows and swallows. He drops the cornbread onto his plate, crumbs scattering. "Should have known. San Francisco. Of course we'd have a vegetarian in the group. I suppose you'd like some avocado toast for breakfast too?"

I glare at him. "You'll have to excuse me for being a

little health-conscious. Have you read the studies about red meat?" My hand drops to the table beside my plate, right where my silverware sits. A spoon launches into the air.

Eddie ducks. "Hey, watch it!" The flying utensil barely misses his head.

"Sorry," I mutter to Eddie, but I can't peel my eyes away from Luca. He's a bit too nice to look at with how his dark waves fall messily but also with undeniable precision. Those eyes, too. How much I want to watch him all evening is a tad disturbing, so I try not to focus on that reaction. He seemed congenial, if a little intrusive, earlier when he walked in on me. Now, he just seems annoyed by my dietary choices. "As I was saying, I try to stick to a healthy diet. High in fiber and low in fat. Red meat doesn't fall into either of those categories."

Grabbing his can of soda, Luca leans back in his chair and takes a big gulp. "So, you probably don't want to know that elk is lower in fat than Salmon by about half."

I pick up my hanging jaw. I don't have the knowledge to counter his point, but it just seems off. Attempting to hide how much he's flustering me, I snap back at him, "Where'd you get that fact? Hunter's Magazine?"

"As a matter of fact—"

"Luca," Emma says in a kind but correcting tone.

He stops talking and glances over. "Sorry, sis." When Emma raises her brows and nods toward me, he adds, "My apologies, Jack. I can be stubborn when it comes to a good debate. Guess it's hard to break those college habits, even after nearly fifteen years."

College? Debate? I can't make the connection between the ranch hand I see here and someone studying rhetoric in college. And sis? He and Emma have absolutely nothing in common physically, so they can't be siblings. Can they? It must be an endearment. Confusing, but why am I worried over it?

"Guess I'll forgive you." I give him a small smirk and reach for the breadbasket he still holds.

He doesn't let go.

"This time," I add.

My boss, Geoffrey, gives me one of his attempts at a smile and looks around Derrick at Luca. "Where did you study?"

Luca makes eye contact, but he doesn't let go of the breadbasket. It's almost as if we're tethered while he answers. "Ivy League, but that's not important. It was a lifetime ago." He lifts one brow.

Ivy League? I scowl. Why's he working on a ranch if he has an Ivy League education? Must not have graduated.

Before I can process much else, he raises his voice, speaking to everyone. "Looks like Jack's got dibs on the bread everyone." Then, his eyes settle on me again, and I fight the urge to demure. "Can't say we bought anything at the store earlier that'd fit your diet requirements. I think we've got some granola bars in the cupboard, though." He lets go, and the basket lurches toward my face. A corn muffin launches into my lap.

I inhale sharply and reach for the bread. With slow deliberation, I close my eyes, steadying myself. A whole week on granola bars and cornbread? Just fantastic. When I open them again, he's staring me down while the others have gone on with conversations and passing plates.

Quietly, I say, "Thanks," and purse my lips. "I suppose."

Luca

WYATT TOSSES IN BED ONCE again and pulls the blanket with him. His bed isn't big enough for the both of us, and if it weren't for Jack turning out to be a woman, I'd be sleeping soundly in my queen-sized bed and soft blankets. Instead, I'm lying here, with nothing more than a sheet, and a grown man next to me not sharing the blanket. Starting tomorrow, I'll be on the hard ground. All I wanted tonight was a good night's sleep.

I glance at my phone on the nightstand and groan when I see the time. I need to be up in three hours to prepare the horses and gear for day one, and I don't think I've slept yet. I jolt upright in bed when I hear something stirring in the hallway. The last time I heard a noise like this was when we were hosting another retreat, and someone went out in the night to relieve themselves. They left the door wide open when they returned, and a pair of raccoons found their way into the kitchen.

I spent hours on end trying to trap the trash pandas and get them back outside, which isn't as easy as it sounds. The people on the retreat thought the entire episode was hilarious, but the incident still haunts me. Sometimes I wake up at night, still convinced we have a raccoon living in our house somewhere. A raccoon that's good at hiding.

There's a clanking noise that sounds like it's coming from the kitchen. I let out a silent sigh, get up, and swipe my jeans from the chair on the other side of the nightstand. In the en suite bathroom, I change out of running shorts into my jeans, and on the way out, I grab a pair of shoes lying on the floor in case I need weapons. The hallway is dark, and I follow the noise, until I see the dim light of the kitchen.

Raccoons don't turn on lights.

I peek around the corner, still ready to meet whatever is behind that door, and I see *her*. She's looking through every cupboard, a heavy sigh coming out of her mouth when she, yet again, doesn't find whatever she's looking for.

I brush my hair off my forehead and lean on the doorjamb. "Can I help you, Jack?"

Startled, she turns to me, and places her hand over her chest as if her heart revved into high gear. Her shoulders drop on the exhalation, and she pats her pink-flushed cheeks. I glance at what she's wearing and shake my head, trying to get myself to quit admiring her tank top and pajama bottoms.

"Why are you here?" Jack says, placing her hands on her hips. "You freaked me out."

"I freaked you out?" I raise both eyebrows. "I thought we were being invaded by raccoons with all the noise coming from this kitchen."

Jack takes another deep breath and relaxes. "I'm sorry." She continues to look around the kitchen. "I'm just going to admit it. I'm starving."

I stroll into the kitchen then and open the refrigerator door. We don't have much that's non-meat or non-dairy, so I glance back at her. "Are you vegan?"

"No, only a pescatarian."

Fish wasn't something I planned to whip up in the middle of the night, so I grab the eggs and hold them up to her with a questioning look. When she nods, I grab some shredded cheese, an onion, and a green pepper too.

"You know," I glance sideways at her, "you could have marked vegetarian on the form you filled out."

"I know," Jack says, shuffling her socked feet. "But I didn't want to seem high maintenance, so I left the field blank. I thought I put in a comment, though."

"We only ask so we can prepare." I crack two eggs into a measuring cup, chop up the ingredients, pour it all into the sizzling pan, and stir the entire time.

"It smells so good," Jack says, pulling herself up onto the island.

When it's done, I put her eggs on a plate and sprinkle them with some salt and pepper. "Here you go."

Jack takes the plate, digs her fork into the eggs, and moans when she takes the first bite. Then, she covers her mouth with one hand as she chews. "Thank you, thank you, thank you," she repeats after swallowing. "These are the best eggs I've ever had. Thank you."

While she eats, I wash and put away the pan. She finishes quickly and I do the same with her plate and fork. Drying my hands on the dish towel, I say, "I have to be up in two hours. You only have three. You should get some sleep. Tomorrow's going to be a long day."

I help her down from the counter and turn to go to bed. I don't make it two steps before I feel her small hand latching onto my arm.

"Thanks again, Luca," Jack says and then pulls on my bicep, so I pause and meet her gaze. There's an unexpected, sparkling curiosity there, and the corners of her lips turn up as she asks, "I'm really curious about your college education."

A tightness forms in my chest, and I'm not sure why. Maybe it's because I'm standing in a kitchen with an undeniably attractive woman in the middle of the night. But I only met her a few hours earlier. Or perhaps the squeeze is because I'd rather talk about anything other than rehashing my life in California.

"There's not much to tell. The most exciting thing I did was win a debate competition," I answer but then I decide I should be a little more cordial about it. I try, but I fear the words still sound snarky. "Let me guess, you're a Berkeley girl?"

"I am!" Jack's eyes widen and she puts her hand over her mouth. "Sorry, I am. How'd you know?"

"Lucky guess." But not that lucky. She fits the profile. Jack looks like she comes from money. Even her pajamas are fancy. Especially compared to my faded and ripped jeans. But she's also someone who seems to care about her urban footprint. Her parents are probably techies or in the medical profession. Granolas who wear Tevas and spend their weekends hiking and picking up trash before returning to their multi-million-dollar home in the hills and sipping expensive Napa Valley wine as they soak their sore muscles in a hot tub overlooking the sea.

Jack washes her hands in the sink. "I'm just surprised to hear you studied at a prestigious school. I mean, most probably rarely make that choice and then end up working on a dude ranch." Jack stretches her arms high above her head, revealing just a sliver of skin at her midsection.

I avert my eyes, knowing I'm entering dangerous territory here. "Well, I'm not like most people." I switch the kitchen light off, and Jack follows me into the hallway. "Now, get to bed. The sun is going to be up before you know it."

When I make it back to Wyatt and Emma's room, I lay on top of the covers, not bothering to remove my jeans. But instead of falling back asleep, I rest my head on my arms, stare at the ceiling, and try to think about anything but Jack.

Chapter Four

Jack

THE ALARM ON MY PHONE starts softly, and I tug my pillow over my head. The jangling sound is nothing, muffled in truth compared to the clanging of metal against metal that begins outside the window. I groan and pull the pillow tighter, pushing the plushness into my ears. The pounding could just be the call to breakfast rather than a real headache, but it's hard to tell with that racket. Today is not the day.

The iron clanging finally ceases, and I call over to Emma. "Can I sleep for one more hour before we have to go? We're really in no rush to get on with this drive."

No reply.

I lift the pillow and peer over to the cot on the other side of the room.

Empty.

Thuds, likely my team members' boots, echo from

the hallway as I drag myself from bed. I don't even look at the time. It's dark. Not an hour when normal human beings are up and eating. When a rooster outside calls for the morning sun, I groan and crawl back under the covers. Everyone has to eat before it'll be time to roll, so I can get another half hour at least. After re-setting the alarm, my eyes drift closed . . . toward some blessed sleep.

The rooster calls again, and it's not the sound we all learned in kindergarten when we all sang "The Farmer in the Dell." Before much longer, a donkey joins the obnoxious chorus. The doorknob clicks and the hinges whine as light floods in from the hallway. Maybe if I'm still, they'll leave.

A second later, someone tugs on the sheets. "You gotta get moving, Jack." Emma's voice cuts through my clouded brain. "We've got breakfast burritos to take along. It's riding and eating at the same time this morning if we're going to keep on schedule."

I moan and roll over, accepting her hand to help me sit upright, and run my fingers through my tangled hair.

Emma looks around at the clothes I've strewn over my open suitcase on the floor in the corner. "Why aren't you packed already?"

"Almost. That bag over there." I wave a hand toward the duffel in the corner and swipe a pair of new jeans I'd laid out for today.

Emma picks up my bag up while I cross to the adjoining bathroom. "There's a lot of stuff still here. What else do you need packed and what can stay behind?"

From the bathroom, I answer. "There's two pairs of

boots. I'll wear the taller ones, but the shorter ones can go in the bag."

Her voice comes back. "Didn't the guidelines say to only bring one pair of shoes for the ride?"

"What if one pair gets messed up? Or I step in—heaven forbid—a pile of manure?"

"It's unlikely. Just take the more comfortable ones and leave the others with the rest of your stuff." I could almost hear her eye roll. "What else?"

"Should I wear the chaps or pack them?" I ask.

"Uh . . ." Emma starts. "Those weren't on the list we sent. You shouldn't need them. Our saddles are plenty comfortable, and we won't be riding into any forests with underbrush. Good denim is enough."

"Oh," I say and grab the toiletry bag sitting on the counter. Stepping out into the room, I lift it in the air. "I hope there's still room in there for this."

One hand holding my bag and the other on her hip, Emma raises her brows. "And that is?"

"Hair dryer. Makeup. Moisturizer. Individual charcoal mask. You know,"I shrug one shoulder, "the essentials."

Emma rolls her lips between her teeth and blinks slowly. "Leave the hair dryer and the mask and bring the rest. Put it all by the door, and we'll get it over to the trading post to go back to the airport with you this weekend. Chaps stay here too. I'll take your bag down."

"Aw, really? But they had those adorable silver studs."

"Yes. Really," she says. It's a little short, but I can tell she's trying to be nice. She turns on her heel to leave. "Five minutes and we're riding out."

I pack my hair dryer in the bag that has to stay behind, hoping wherever we're stopping for the night will have one I can use. After sliding on my new boots, I sling my essentials bag over one shoulder and follow Emma into the hall, yawning. "Is there coffee?"

"We'll stop about two hours in for coffee on the trail."

"What?" I groan and watch my feet as we walk, uncertain if I'll stumble in the huge boots. The pointy toes stick out well beyond any of the normal shoes in my wardrobe. I seriously don't know how people wear these on a regular basis. The lack of coffee is a real problem, though! My head might explode if I don't get my morning dose of caffeine, especially after being up in the middle of the night hungry and with Luca. Heat flushes into my cheeks, and I smile. There's something about that cowboy that seems a little out of place. Maybe trying to puzzle that out will get me through the first couple of hours.

Out front of the ranch house, Emma tosses my bag to Luca, who eyes me as if I'm going to be the bane of his existence on this trip. He even does the one-brow quirk at me as I step forward, thinking how irritation looks good on him. Everything does. As my foot lowers onto the first step, he tips his hat, and I quickly forget how to walk. My left foot is too far forward when I place it, so I slip down the next three steps and land on my tush with my boots in the air. Luca covers his mouth, hiding a laugh, and turns toward one of the largest horses in the bunch with my bag in hand.

My jaw gapes open. He was so nice last night, so it seems odd that he is hostile and rude this morning. Whatever. I guess my hunger kept him from getting his beauty sleep too. All the horses are lined up on one side, saddled. Luca drops my bag next to one that has a gorgeous sable and white coat and promptly empties the contents into the saddlebags. Heat flushes my face as he handles my clothes—undergarments and all. All I have time to do is watch helplessly from the ground, because he's closing the flap before I can object. He hangs the designer bag on the fencepost behind him and moves on to tending the next horse.

Emma looks over her shoulder and turns back to help me off the ground. "Getting a little dusty already, I see." She smiles warmly and pulls me to my feet.

"I swear, Emma, I'm usually not this uncoordinated."

My teammates stand in a huddle, looking at the line of animals, and whisper among themselves. Fortunately, I don't think any of them noticed me biff it on the stairs. Bruce has a trekking pole at his side, leaning his weight onto it. I almost wish he hadn't come, given the newness of his hip, but he insisted it'd be fine. I hop he'll be able to straddle the horse. At least he signed the waivers.

Eddie waves and I cross the front lawn to stand by his side.

"You're lookin' like the cheese fell off your cracker, doll face." He looks me up and down and shoots me his classic narrow-eyed, pursed-lips, challenging stare.

"Wha—" I scowl and shake my head when the meaning sets in. "I didn't get to sleep until late. Had to find something to eat in this carnivore haven."

"Oh? And?" he drawled.

"Luca cooked some eggs." I tuck my hair behind one ear.

Eddie's mouth drops open and his eyes go round. He's about to say something, but—

"Gather 'round!" Wyatt waves his hands to pull us into a semicircle, and we fall into formation.

Eddie recovers himself but drawls a suggestive "Mm-hmm" as we move closer.

Wyatt flips through papers on his clipboard. "Nine of you and three of us. I'll take Sean, Nathan, and Bruce. Anthony, Derrick, and Geoffrey, you'll work with Emma. Calvin, Eddie, Jack, you're with Luca."

"Hold up there, Wyatt." Luca rushes over and whispers just loud enough for me to hear. "Don't you think Jack should go with Emma?"

I grind my teeth. So, apparently, Luca is just as sexist as any of my teammates. I didn't peg him for that, but I'm taking copious mental notes now.

Wyatt snorts and claps Luca on the shoulder. "Get 'em saddled up." He takes his three. Emma waves to her group, and the rest of us join Luca.

"All right, here's the deal. We've got five full days before we reach the Gilbert Trading Post with the cattle. We could do it in three, but because this is a corporate retreat, we break it up with some team-building activities." He looks at me and snorts.

I inhale sharply, covering my chest with one hand. "I'm not sure what you mean by that, but I'll have you know that I'm excellent with team building. I'm the one who organized this trip, so I know what I'm in for." What I don't say is . . . at least I hope I do.

He leans one arm onto the sable-colored horse's saddle and crosses one foot over the other. My eyes trail down his long legs, over the jeans hugging muscular thighs and calves, and to the dusty boots he wears.

After a short stare-off, he says, "Is that so?" and gives me the same once-over, and my body flushes with heat where his eyes roam.

Ignore it, I tell myself and answer, "It is." I nod once as if to put a period on the statement.

"Then perhaps you can show us how to mount up with Jasper here." Luca steps to the side, holding out one hand for me—be my guest style.

Luca

I WAS PLANNING TO RIDE Jasper myself, but Jack has been acting so arrogant since her arrival, I pulled an audible and assigned him to her. Jasper is one of our taller horses, and I smirk as Jack puts her left foot in the strap and tries to throw her right leg over. She falls short and comes crashing down. It's her second time in the dirt this morning, and I can't help how ironic I find her entire situation.

I cover my mouth with one hand, trying desperately to hide the laugh threatening to bellow from my lips. "Did you tighten the saddle? It looks a little loose."

Jack stands up, brushes the grass off of her jeans, and

looks up at me. "I assumed you had taken care of the saddle before I risked my life trying to get on the horse."

She stands with her hands planted on her hips, clearly as annoyed with me as I am with her. Although, unlike me, she doesn't seem to find any humor in the situation, which makes me want to laugh even more. I concede and help her off the ground. This time, she accepts my help, following my lead as I approach Jasper.

"I put the saddle on, but before you hop on, always make sure the saddle is tight. Here, like this." I pull to tighten the strap against Jasper's side.

This gorgeous gelding stands patiently waiting for us to get this right, and I whisper a little praise in his ear as I finish up. I drop the strap and let Jack take it. She's so short her head barely reaches the horse's back.

"Do you want to try again?" I ask her.

Jack bites her lip, looks up at Jasper, down to the ground, and then at me. She looks scared, and I feel like a jerk because I'm not making this any easier. But when she acts like a know it all, I can't help myself. Perhaps it's the constant sports I played during high school or the debate team I was part of in college, but my competitive side claws its way to the surface where she's concerned. I want to show her that she's not as great as she thinks she is. But when she shows any hint of vulnerability, I find myself wanting to run and rescue her.

This is all extremely confusing.

"Here," I point to the foot strap and step up behind her. "Let me help you."

She hesitates but then puts her foot in the strap and

stretches up to grab the horn of the saddle.

I settle my hands at her waist, ready to give her a little help in launching from the ground, and her head whips around to look up at me. I fight a confused reaction: back off or hold on tighter? Breathing deeply, I look up toward the saddle and try to focus on the task rather than how her midsection feels between my palms. "Now," I say. "Put all of your strength in swinging your leg over. I'll give you an extra push."

Jack nods and then pushes her weight into the stirrup. As she swings her leg over, I instinctively give her a push on her rear end with my hand to make sure she clears Jasper. Her leg flies over the horse, and I jerk my hand back, regretting it.

"Uh, I'm s—sorry about that."

She brushes me off with a wave. "It's fine. I'm on the horse. Isn't that right, Jasper?" Looking a little too self-satisfied, Jack pats Jasper on the neck.

What's surprising to me is how he leans into her touch, not at all bothered that someone other than me is riding him for the first time in a while.

Calvin and Eddie are already on their horses, chatting away and smiling. Calvin is telling Eddie about his twin eight-year-old daughters and how they've just gotten into competitive dancing. "At this rate," he says, "I won't have the money to send them to college."

Eddie gives him a cheerleading-type reply, "You're young and have a fab job. You and Darla will get there soon enough. By the time they're eighteen, I'm sure *you'll be walkin' in high cotton.*"

I swallow a laugh at hearing Eddie's thesaurus of southern phrases put to good use. I have a feeling he and Calvin will be the low maintenance members of my group. I finish strapping the bags to our horses. Once everyone is on their horses, I hop on Lucy, my mare, and we start down the path.

By the time we start on the trail toward Gilbert Trading Post, the sun is high in the sky. I grab my hat from the satchel on the side of the horse and pull it low on my head. Wyatt's group leads the charge, followed by Emma and her three, and my group brings up the rear. Calvin acts like he knows what he's doing, and Eddie rides directly behind him, followed by Jack, who looks nervous but seems to hold her own. I ride directly behind her.

For not being experienced, Jack's riding posture isn't half bad. She bears her weight in the stirrups when Jasper speeds to a canter as if she's been in a saddle before. I can hear her talking to him too, but she's speaking too quietly for me to make out what she's saying.

"Hey, guys," I call out. "In about another mile, the trail opens up to a field. Your horse's instinct will be to gallop, so unless you want to take flight across these plains, you're going to have to keep a tight hold on the reins."

Calvin and Eddie nod their heads in acknowledgment, but Jack doesn't even flinch.

"Did you catch that?" I say to the back of Jack's head.

"Yep, I heard you. Pull back on the reins. Got it." Although she doesn't bother to glance in my direction, I can practically hear the eye roll in her voice.

The trail surrounded by trees and brush starts to open up. I pull my hat off to wipe my brow and then put it back on. The dirt trail turns into an expansive field of sagebrush. Jasper kicks up his front legs. I've seen that move a hundred times before, so my stomach lodges itself in my throat. There's no time to say a word before Jasper takes off in a full speed gallop.

Jack grabs his reins and screams—a blood-curdling sound. From what I can see, she doesn't try to pull back and, instead, appears completely frozen with the reins loose. I kick the side of my horse and try to catch up with Jasper, but he's one of our fastest horses.

"Pull back on the reins," I yell, but my volume isn't matching Jack's hysteric screams. "Pull back, Jack!" I say with more urgency.

I catch up and, with my left hand, grab part of Jasper's rein. "Whoa, Jasper, Whoa," I say again, keeping my tone low and steady but calm. Exactly the tone I've used over the last couple of years while training him.

Jasper slows to a trot then comes to a complete halt. All of the color has drained out of Jack's face, and she's shaking a little. I open my mouth to tell her how to properly dismount, but she flings her leg over Jasper's neck and slides out of the saddle. To her luck, he's focused on me at the moment and doesn't make a move to dart.

She paces back and forth, running her hands through her dark brown hair, and I dismount from Lucy.

"I'm never getting on a horse again! Ever. Done. Never." She pins me with an angry glare. "I thought you had them trained better than that?" She flips her hand angrily toward Jasper. "Your website says the horses are all trained to be gentle with the riders. I could have died!"

"You're fine. You're going to be okay," I try to reassure her. "And Thoroughgood horses *are* the best trained in New Mexico."

She huffs, crosses her arms, and quirks a brow at me.

Dang, I really don't like how adorable I find her pout.

"That is a devil of a horse," she says. "I'm never getting back on him."

Jasper takes his head and rubs it against my hand, and the need to protect him swells in my chest. Jasper is the best horse I've ever ridden. I try to hold my voice steady through my clenched teeth. "If you would have followed instructions, this wouldn't have happened. This is on you, Jack. Not Jasper."

"But—" Jack says.

I cut her off. "I warned you that a horse's instinct is to run in open spaces. Like most other relationships, riding a horse is a partnership. You have to give him instructions appropriately."

Calvin circles his horse around where we're standing and comes to a stop. "You're fine, Jack. Quit being dramatic."

Jack glares at him. "Is that how you calm your girls, Cal?"

He looks down at the saddle horn and sighs. Apparently, she's tough for others on her team to deal with too.

Eddie can't stop laughing. "I've never heard anyone scream like that." He grabs his side. "Never thought I'd see that side of you." He laughs even harder.

"It's not funny," Jack says, but there's a twitch at the corners of her mouth. She's the center of attention right now, and apparently that's lifting her mood just a little, even if she doesn't want to admit it.

"I'm not joking," she insists. "I'm not getting back on the horse. Not doing it. Even if he is the best horse ever. As you so eloquently put it."

Wyatt and Emma's groups are barely visible anymore, as they've finished crossing open field, and are back on the trail at the other end.

"Well, our policy is no man, or woman," I cough, "left behind, and we've gone too far to have the entire group turn back."

Jack looks at me, sheer panic on her face, and I know she isn't joking. Jasper running at almost full speed freaked her out, something I hadn't expected after how comfortable and capable she seemed initially in the saddle. Jack strikes me as someone who always has to be in control. And nothing makes us feel like we have less control than riding a seven-hundred-pound animal who has his mind set on running.

Calvin and Eddie grow impatient, watching the others move farther away and moving their horses a little in their direction.

I look at Jack and know there is nothing I can say to get her back on a horse by herself right now. "You're going to have to ride with me then. Jack pauses, lips pursed, and then says, "Fine."

Jasper is bigger than Lucy, so I hop on him, and then

hold my hand out to Jack.

She stares at my hand as if it's a snake. "Why not Lucy?"

"She's not big enough to bear the weight."

It takes Jack another solid minute to accept my hand. After I help her up, she sits on the saddle in front of me, and there's no space to keep any sort of distance. My legs rub against her hips, and I can't do anything about it. "Here. Hold his reins for a sec while I tie off Lucy."

Jack inhales sharply, but doesn't take the reins from my hand.

"He won't go anywhere with me on here. I'll try to show you a thing or two so you can get back to riding comfortably. But I need to tether Lucy, or she might head back to the ranch."

"I—"

"You will," I cut her off. "Eventually."

I tie Lucy's reins around the horn of Jasper's saddle, slide my hand over Jack's, and slip the leather from her grasp. Jack looks around struggling where to hold on.

"Here," I answer her unspoken question. "Either put your hand on the horn or grab Jasper's mane. It doesn't hurt him." I don't tell her that she doesn't need to hold on or that she likely won't fall off while she's wedged into my torso with my arms and legs cocooning her.

Jack sits up taller and laces her fingers into Jasper's black mane. It seems to give her a little reassurance, so that's one win. Her other hand shares the horn with me, fingers close enough I can feel the heat coming from them. Tearing my mind away from that sensation is torturous, but I need to ignore the electricity jumping back and forth between our hands.

I lead Jasper and Lucy and the rest of my group onward. We catch up to the others and ride in silence for what feels like forever before I finally decide to break the ice. "You need to let Jasper know what you want him to do. Horses can sense your fear, so you shouldn't let them feel it."

Jack's body relaxes against mine, only slightly. "I literally thought I was going to die."

"Jasper is still a young man," I say. "He needs to know you're in control."

"I didn't feel in control," Jack says, straightening her back.

"Then you have to fake it," I say. "Jasper needs to trust you just as much as you need to trust him, and he trusts confidence in his rider."

Horses are so much less complicated than humans. Jasper requires so little from us aside from solid guidance. Some love, some trust, and the rest usually falls into place.

"Okay, while I have you here," I continue, "let's practice how to give Jasper commands with your body, because you are going to get back in the saddle, so to speak."

Jack glances back at me. There is no room to move away or be anywhere but plastered to her back. It's only a moment that her breath brushes against my neck and then she looks forward again. "Fine. Tell me everything I need to know."

A wall seems to drop and I take the opportunity. I take Jack's hand in mine and place one rein inside, still holding onto the end myself. Then I do the same with the other.

"We're going to get Jasper into a trot and then I'll show you how to stop him. First, press into both his sides with your heels. Not too hard. And definitely not a kick." I wait for her to follow my instructions, unsure if she's even breathing.

"You're going to be fine. I'm right here to stop him if he runs."

Jack

WHAT IN THE WORLD AM I doing? Why did I choose a cattle drive—of all things—for our team outing? Everyone else, including Eddie, seems perfectly comfortable with their horses. So, why did I end up with a wild beast? I wonder for a second if it was Luca's intent to ride with me all along. But the suspicion evaporates almost as soon as it sparks, because for some annoying reason, I do feel better about riding with him surrounding me like this.

Geez, Jack. Not the point.

I focus on the situation and lesson Luca's trying to teach me, still irritated that my summer at horse camp didn't prepare me for this. The fact that I'd reacted so strongly to the misogyny at work also niggled into the back of my neck. Mari, while I love her spunk, is going to get a piece of my mind as soon as we stop for the night. I hope my phone will still have a charge by then. And I hope the accommodation allows for a nice, warm bath.

After that jaunt and sliding down the steps earlier, my tush needs a good soaking.

"Jack? You still here?" Luca's voice brings me out of my head.

"Yeah. Sorry. What?"

"Give Jasper a little squeeze with your heels. Gently. He'll canter, but don't panic. I've got you." His arm comes around my waist, and I jerk.

My breath is clogged in my throat, so I grunt to clear it and look down at his arm. "What are you doing?"

"We don't have two sets of stirrups. So, I'm going to lift you from the saddle when you get Jasper into a canter. I thought you knew this by how you began the ride."

Something from my preteen horse camps triggered. "Yeah. Guess I did . . . or at least my muscles did."

"Ready?" he asks encouragingly.

A feeling of safety washes through me, as if he'll protect me from the jarring danger I felt when the horse leaped into a run before. I nod, squeeze my heels, gasp, and grab the reins tighter as Jasper begins to trot.

The muscles in Luca's legs stiffen until they're as hard as rocks and he lifts me off the saddle. "Now, you hover in the saddle with your weight on your feet. And, most importantly, stay calm."

I'm holding my breath, praying he'll stop Jasper before the insane horse bolts down the trail.

"And breathe, Jack! Keep breathing or you'll pass out."

With his command, my lungs expand, and the oxygen helps slow my racing heart.

"The ride is always rougher between walking and a full-on run. When the horse is running at higher speeds, the ride is actually smooth."

"O—okay." But I don't want to do that, regardless of how much I feel Luca has complete control over the situation. "Smooth is nice, but can we go back to slow-mo now?"

He chuckles in my ear, and his breath is warm, sending chills down my spine. "Yeah. Pull the reins toward you gently and say, 'Whoa.'"

I follow his instructions, and amazingly, Jasper slows. Luca lowers me down to the saddle and removes his arm. My waist suddenly feels cold.

The group ahead of us veers to the left, and Luca says in my ear, "Now, to ask Jasper to turn left, press your right knee softly into his side."

A smile spreads across my face when I do and the horse does exactly what I wanted. Maybe I will get the hang of this after all.

We enter a small clearing and Wyatt holds up his arm, hand fisted. "Who's ready for coffee?"

My mouth waters immediately, and my head pounds. Me. Most definitely.

Chapter Five

IN THE CLEARING, WE DIRECT the LivFit team to circle the herd in order to keep them calm while we take a break for coffee. When everything is settled, I whistle for Frankie, the cattle dog, to come heel. She perks her ears, tail up, and trots alongside Lucy as we return to the rest of the group.

Jack stands at Jasper's side, where I left her with a little black bag in her hand. As annoyed as I was starting out the day, riding with Jack was a great reminder of why I moved here to begin with. The open air and learning to see nature and animals in new ways settles my heart. My mind doesn't race here like it did in the city. I don't enjoy seeing anyone scared to ride these beautiful animals, but to watch Jack conquer her fear, gain confidence, and develop a quiet poise with Jasper made my day. That calming of the soul she's displaying now is my reason.

This city girl with ladder-climbing aspirations and

the change I see in her paint the perfect picture of my *why*.

Eddie, the young and energetic member of the LivFit team, comes over to where I'm standing with a huge, exhilarated grin on his face. "I'm surprised we're stopping already. We've only been riding a couple of hours. I could go on forever." He isn't experiencing this adventure the same way as Jack. This is a new thrill for him, a novelty, whereas Jack has the characteristic off-kilter manner of someone who could come to enjoy this life. The thought sends a shudder through me, and I gasp as if I hadn't been breathing. They're clients. This is my job. I need to keep everything here professional.

Their colleague, Bruce, approaches us and crosses his arms over his chest. "Eddie, would you quit being so eager? It's about time we stopped. I can't feel my left butt cheek." To emphasize the fact, he lets his left hand drift down and grimaces. If I recall correctly, he is the one who just had his hip replaced.

"Hey, I brought my French press," Jack says as she walks close to where Emma is getting ready to start the fire. Jack opens a little black bag with what looks like a silk drawstring and draws out pulls a campground sized press. Her eyes twinkle like she's just solved everyone's problems for the day, but I stare at the dainty thing in astonishment. Of all the things to bring, she prioritized that?

"Who wants to help get the fire started?" Emma asks. She looks over this retreat group like a proud mom teaching her children something new. "Bruce, why don't you give it a go?"

Bruce lets out a huff but walks over to the firepit and Emma shows him what to do. I check on the horses, and Jack approaches me.

"Not a bad idea on the French press, right?" she says with a large smile on her face.

I strain my neck to look over my shoulder and down at her. A few sarcastic comments come to mind, but Jack seems too proud of herself for me to let any of those fly.

I chuckle and pat her on the shoulder. "You did good, Jack. This will be the first retreat where we actually have good coffee."

Yeah, it's an odd choice of something to bring, but I won't deny that the quality of coffee it'll make is far superior to the chewy stuff out of the percolator. And decent coffee after the sleepless night might hit the spot. We stand around, all sipping on the coffee, and Wyatt explains the upcoming four-hour trek, mostly uphill, until we reach the place we'll settle for the night.

When all the questions die away and almost everyone has put away their coffee mugs, Wyatt calls, "Okay team, let's pack up our stuff, check the horses, and get back on the trails. Our next leg is long."

My eyes follow Jack, as she proudly stows her coffee maker into her bag. I continue to follow her as she stands in front of Jasper, and a nervous look crosses her face.

I finish packing up the remainder of our things into my bag and then walk over to her. "You ready to ride solo?"

Jack scrapes her lip between her teeth. "I mean, I think I'm ready, but I'm nervous too," she admits.

I hold the saddle steady, and guide Jack's leg into the stirrup. "Remember what I told you, and everything will be fine. You've got this. Jasper is more scared of you than you'll ever be of him. Get him to trust you. Be his friend."

"You make it sound so easy," she says.

Jack presses down on the stirrup and swings her other leg over the saddle, easier this time. When Jasper turns his head, Jack affectionately strokes his neck. I go back to Lucy, but my eyes never leave her.

"See, it's that easy," I say.

Someone coughs behind me, and I peer over my shoulder to see Emma. She smiles at me, loops her arm in mine, and lowers her voice to a point where I almost can't hear her clearly. "Jack really seems to be getting the hang of this."

"Yeah, well, she should." I infuse as much feigned sarcasm as possible into my words. "I spent all morning giving her instructions." I throw in an eye roll for good measure.

Emma laughs and punches me lightly on the shoulder. "Ah, yes. It definitely seems like you *hated* that, Luca. You know . . . my favorite romance novels have this pattern thingy where there's only one horse." Both her eyebrows shoot up toward her hairline.

"Hey, I'm just being a team player." I press my palm toward her in a stop-right-there gesture to stop her train of thought on the spot. "This is business, and I'm only helping one of our clients."

Emma pats my horse, and as she walks away, she turns and gives me *the look*. Yes, the one that seems far too motherly. "Be careful, Luca. We don't want to get too attached to these retreat goers. Remember what happened with that summer hand we had. What was his name?"

"Elliot?" A look of remembrance spreads across my face. That entire situation was a disaster.

Emma snaps and points at me. "Yup. He was worthless at driving the herd once he became infatuated with that girl on the youth retreat."

I suspect Emma knew his name all along and just made me come up with it to emphasize her point. But she's right. "True," I say, musing. "And I had to pull him out of that girl Sophie's tent more than once." I get up on my horse, meaning to follow Jack so I can supervise. "I get the message, Emma. Loud and clear."

Emma rubs her nose, still eying me suspiciously. "That was a youth retreat, though . . . You're a big boy, Luca. I won't be pulling you out of anyone's tent."

"I can guarantee you won't be," I say with finality.

She's right, I need to focus more on the group and less on Jack. As hard as that will be.

Jack

LUCA IGNORES ME ENTIRELY FOR the remainder of the day, and I'm confused. Again. He's so hot and cold. He was helpful earlier, and I was getting a little nervous flutter in my stomach every time our hands brushed on the reins while he rode Jasper behind me. But his coaching had done the trick, and everything I learned as a kiddo in horse camp miraculously came flooding back.

Through the afternoon, riding comes more naturally, and I'm in love with Jasper by the time Wyatt directs everyone to a roundup the herd for the day. I only watched before, but I join in this time, and my heart races as I urge Jasper into a canter. He also follows the patterns of the other horses and riders, and it's easy to steer him with just a little pressure on one knee or the other.

When the cows have come to a stop, Wyatt waves all the LivFit employees over to one side. Emma and Luca remain on the far side of the herd with the cattle dog Frankie. Our team, still on horseback, gathers into a huddle near a small copse of trees. The herd is some distance away, nearing a pen made from logs—the kind I remember from the old westerns my dad made me watch when I was a kid. This experience definitely has a *Rawhide* feel, and despite myself and my corporate, city-girl attitude, I'm growing quite nostalgic.

Wyatt puts his little fingers in the corners of his mouth and whistles. I wince and shove my palm against my ear that faces his direction as the sound pierces my senses. When the long shrill is done, the two border collies Butch and Cassidy dart out of the cluster of trees and circle around the cows, moving them into a tighter group. It's fascinating to watch two riders and three dogs work as a team to move the cattle toward the pen.

"Ya'll wait here while we corral them for the night." Wyatt leaves the group to join the others working the herd. Emma and Luca dig their heels into the sides of their steeds and lash their haunches with the length of their reins. Suddenly, I forget about Wyatt, Emma, and the dogs and become enthralled with Luca's form as he leans into the mare.

A hand with a red and white bandana enters my peripheral vision, and I feel another horse brush against my leg.

"Here. You might want to wipe up that stream of drool," says Eddie. "*You look like you just fell off the turnip truck.*"

"I am not drooling over that neanderthal," I say, but betraying my words, my hand lifts idly to make sure of the fact.

Eddie laughs. "There's nothing wrong with admiring that *fine* specimen of a man."

I don't like the hungry look on Eddie's face or the way he drawls *fine*. I school my expression, though, and continue observing the herding activities. Wyatt drops one log of the pen while Luca, Emma, Butch, Cassidy, and Frankie drive the cows inside.

"Girl," Eddie interrupts my intense study of the scene, "you can wipe the jealousy off your face. Luca's been sizing you up too."

"No way." I scowl.

"Yes, way. You're just not looking when he does."

Our hosts finish up and trot their horses back to our group.

"So . . ." Wyatt swipes his cowboy hat off his head and runs a hand over his balding head. "Now that you've seen it, we'll take three volunteers to pen up the cows tomorrow."

Eddie's hand shoots up, and I smile. No one else is

quick to volunteer, and I'm leery of going first too.

"C'mon," Luca says, "everyone will get the chance. We just need the first three."

Sean pipes up with an exaggerated drawl, "Ah, heck. I'll give it a go too." He's getting into the role, and that makes me smile.

"One more," says Emma. "We'll help, but this is one of the team-building activities you'll reflect on at the end of the retreat."

I open my mouth to nominate our boss Geoffrey when—

"Thanks, Jack!" Luca cuts me off.

"I was going to say . . ." I narrow my eyes at the smirking cowboy. "I think Geoffrey, as our leader, should go first."

Emma guides her horse between me and Luca, looking at him. I can't see her face or if she says anything to him silently, but he shrinks a little in the saddle.

"Awesome!" Emma says. "So, we have Jack, Sean, and Eddie for tomorrow. For now, shall we get camp set up?"

Wyatt slides off his horse, scratching Butch behind his black ear. The black and white Border Collie with one blue eye leans into Wyatt's touch and groans audibly.

After everyone dismounts, Wyatt frees a leather strap with some metal rings and a buckle from his saddle and holds it up. "Everyone should have one of these on your saddles. Time to learn to hobble the horses."

My heart skips, and I unintentionally shoot a wide-eyed glance over to Luca.

He tips his hat, hiding his eyes, grabs the strap from his mare's saddle, and bends down to her side near her hooves.

Wyatt holds the strap up. "This is called a figure eight hobble." He crouches in front of his horse. "Run it behind and around the outside leg, loop it through the ring in both directions, and around the inside leg and buckle it off. Make sure you keep it loose. The horses are trained to graze in a small circle with these on, but you don't want it too tight." He finishes and stands. "Now, you all give it a whirl."

Luca and Emma finished hobbling their own horses by the time Wyatt said this.

"We're here to assist if you need help," Emma adds.

Before I crouch to put the strap around Jasper's legs, I work it into the figure eight. When it seems to make sense, I bend down and follow Wyatt's instructions to a tee. When I finish, it looks exactly like Wyatt's work, so I stand up and hold my hands out as if it was the easiest thing in the world. In front of Jasper, I hold his reins in one hand and stroke his soft muzzle with the other.

"Once you've got the hobble in place," says Wyatt, "you're going to lead your horse to his or her left like this." Luca gently pulls the reign in the direction he wants the horse to go.

Still in front of my horse, I use my left hand to push slightly on Jasper's muzzle to get him to turn. He stumbles and rears up on his hind legs, and before I can process what's happening, I'm prone on the ground, boots in the air for the second time in one day. I sit up, drape my arms over my knees, and let my head hang between my arms. Why am I the only one having such a hard time with this? I breathe slowly, attempting to quell my embarrassment, and see Luca's boots jogging over to the horse.

"Whoa, boy. Whoa." Luca's voice soothes Jasper and I peek over to see what's going on.

Luca has settled Jasper and smiles. He looks down at me and laughs.

Luca

I OFFER JACK A HAND and try desperately to curb my laughter. But I'm hopeless when it comes to pretending. The corners of my mouth hurt from trying to fight the smile. I rub my nose with my free hand; maybe that'll cover it.

"You, um, yeah. You can't stand in front of a horse while guiding them. Their eyes are on the sides of their head, so they can't see you and don't understand what's happening."

"You don't have to be so amused at my ignorance," she chides. And, really, how adorable is her irritation?

I attempt to divert my eyes away from Jack as she brushes dirt off her pants. It's pointless, though. I can't help but follow the path her hands trace over her curves. Her face is red with embarrassment, and she looks everywhere but at me.

I chuckle to myself and then return to my horse. I can't forget the job to be done. "Alright guys, the sun is getting low, so we don't have a lot of time to get camp set up. We want to make it there and have all the tents pitched before nightfall."

"We're not camping here?" Someone groans, and I look back but don't see who says it.

"Day one is always the longest," Wyatt calls out. "The rest of the days there will be less action and movement. I promise."

There are a few groans from the group, but we all grab our bag and tents from the horses and start walking along a smaller trail. I'm bringing up the rear, following Jack again. Everyone is walking a little stiffly, and Jack's limping a little. I hope she didn't hurt herself when she fell. She stops and wipes something off her boot heel and then continues on, no longer favoring the one leg. Good.

The first full day is always the hardest for every group. Horseback riding is physical, and it's not easy being out in the sun all day. I'm proud of this team, though. They've been marching along, almost without complaint. I'm even proud of Jack and her turnaround.

The sun continues to head west, and the air gets slightly cooler, which is a welcomed break from how scorching it's been all day.

"See that landing up ahead?" I say to no one in particular, but Jack turns around at the sound of my voice. "That's where we'll settle for the night."

Jack's whole-body sigh of relief is immediate.

"Okay, everyone," Emma says. "Pick a place around the perimeter where you'll pitch your tent. Fire will be in the middle."

"Once ya'll are done," Wyatt chimes in, "we'll need someone to get a fire started, so we can start cooking dinner."

"And we can't forget about the cattle," Emma calls out. "We'll all need to watch them, but they usually stay put near the water's edge."

I drop my gear near a tree and untie the water jugs from my bags.

Apparently, Emma is thinking the same thing, because she calls out, "I'm going to go down to the brook and fill some water jugs. Any volunteers to come?"

"No use *burnin' daylight*," Eddie says first.

Strolling over to him, I thrust the two jugs I'm carrying into his chest. He grins and accepts them and then follows Emma to the water.

I return to my chosen camp spot, extract the camping tent from my bag, and roll it out near the tree. I've pitched this tent in this spot over a hundred times, and each time, it gets easier. I could do it in my sleep. The trick is to make sure I avoid the shallow roots. Sleeping on those would cause lots of pain while riding. It's happened before, so I'm always careful to position the tent at a bit of an angle, the entrance facing away from the fire. My spot is a little behind the other tents, so I have a bit of privacy, and it offers recluse from the early morning sun.

The LivFit group pairs off, and most of them are pretty proficient with their tents. Some read instructions but get through the setup with ease. Tent after tent is erected, and a few even seem more adept at it than me. Geoffrey, the boss of the group, and Nathan get theirs up first and set up Eddie's since he went to the stream with Emma. Then, they start on the fire.

Jack stands in front of her tent, which is nothing more than a lump on the ground. Her one arm is across her body, as her other hand holds the directions. After a second, she turns them upside down as if it'll help her get the picture clearer.

I clear my throat. "Need a hand?"

She waves me off.

One after another, everyone finishes pitching their tents, except Jack. A few of her colleagues also try to help, but she refuses every single offer.

Eddie and Emma return with the water and start setting the pot to heat over the fire with the boss's help. Once the pot is secured, Eddie thanks Geoffrey for pitching his tent and goes over to unpack.

I watch the happenings around camp, waiting for Jack to relent with her stubbornness and snicker under my breath when she finally figures out she needs to spread the tent flat on the ground. As she pulls the corners to a flat square, she's got it upside down. I shake my head, wishing that, just for once, there was one of these career-driven women who would ask for help when they needed it.

I move closer. "Jack, you know it is okay to accept help. Let me show you where you're going wrong."

"Please, Luca. I've got this." She points to one diagram, and her erred confidence shines proudly on her face. "See?"

I raise my brows and hold up my hands, taking a step back. As much as I want to, I don't intervene. Instead, I tend to the other camp duties, unpacking the food and assisting Emma where she needs help.

There's a sudden, loud squeal and a *harrumph* from behind me, and I spin around on one heel. Jack's legs flail as she lies under her collapsed tent. Her colleagues don't seem too concerned. In fact, a couple of them snigger like mean girls in grade school. I glare at them as I grab one of the battery-powered lanterns and stride over to give her a hand. This time, I'm not taking no for an answer, but I'm also laughing internally the entire time.

I lift the tent up, and Jack props herself back on one elbow. She pushes her hair out of her eyes and looks up at me with the biggest doe-eyed, or maybe deer-in-the-headlights, look I've ever seen. She lets out a long sigh, sits upright, and hangs her head.

I laugh aloud then. This time, she seems too frustrated over the situation to worry about how humorous I find the situation. "Are you okay?" I manage to ask as I move inside and press the roof of the tent upward.

Jack rests her arms on her knees, looking utterly defeated.

"Here," I say and offer her the lantern. "Hold this."

She takes it from my hand and gives me a small smile, and it may be the first sweet look I've seen her give. I kneel to fix the twisted tent pole, and she says, "I guess I can see why you find this so amusing." Her voice is a bit at ease, perhaps because the others can't see her or us inside the tent. But they can see shadows, so I stick to the work at hand.

Jack lets out a puff of air, and in my periphery, I see her hair fluff out with her breath.

I snap the last pole into place and remind myself of the tactics people are supposed to use in Corporate America. Unfortunately, I remember those days all too well. But . . . maybe a few encouraging words will soothe her a bit.

"You almost had it. There." I give the structure a small tug to show that it's sound and sit down with my legs crossed in front of her. Then, I can't say why, but I get a little truthful. "I find your stubbornness amusing, Jack. On most corporate busy bodies, I find it entirely annoying, but with you, "I pick a burr off my pants leg and shrug, "it's kinda cute."

Her face immediately turns red. Splotches appear on her neck.

So, I backtrack. "Why do you refuse help?" I ask.

"I hate failure," she offers, and there is something serious in her face as she looks at me.

We stare at each other for what feels like forever. Or maybe it feels like just a flash.

Then, suddenly, she glances away. "Look out there." She points to the tent's opening. "Every guy I work with was able to get their tent up. I work on a team with all men, and I have to work twice as hard to prove my worth. In the boardroom, I can keep up with them, no problem, and they still treat me like a second-class citizen."

She screws up her face and mimics someone or maybe more than one person. *Jack, plan a retreat for the team.* "Then, she raises her brows and puts on this ultra-placid mask. *"Jack, why don't you order the food for the team meeting?"* She seems to be speaking from experience, and that explains a lot. *"Jack, our coffee is low. Could you make a fresh pot?"*

"It's just so much work." Jack plops her elbows on her knees and rests her face in her hands. "But out here, I feel like they're all laughing at me, and the whole situation is all my fault. I wanted to get back at them by scheduling this—this . . . outing. But it's totally backfired, and I'm the one out of sorts. Now, everyone is reveling in my failure. I hate that this stuff doesn't come naturally to me."

I study Jack's face and find myself questioning the picture I had painted of her in my mind. A prissy girl, who spends her Saturday mornings drinking expensive coffee, eating scones, and then going to her overly priced Pilates class. I hadn't considered how hard it must be to prove herself repeatedly with all the male energy from her colleagues.

"A word of advice," I offer.

Jack's eyes dart up to meet mine and her posture stiffens.

For a split second, I wonder if she lumps me into the same boat as her peers and boss. Probably. Feeling chagrin over judging her so coldly, I hold up my hands—a tiny apology. "That is, if I may?"

She nods.

"You're just as talented as everyone out there. Probably more than most. You don't have to be good at everything in the world. And you're sitting in a tent with someone who has both lived their game and knows his way around camping. Asking for and accepting help doesn't show weakness."

"Well, maybe to you," Jack responds, but then she sighs and backpedals. "Yeah. You're probably right."

I'm not ready to spill my story to a total stranger. And one who will be gone in a week, to boot. "Did you really watch them, Jack?"

"Watch who?" she asks.

When she looks at me, her eyebrows pull together.

"Your colleagues. Not one of them put their tents up alone. They helped each other. Trusted one another. And that's why they got it done quickly. You're trying to do it on your own, but that rarely works out the best."

She furrows her brows. What I said seems to make her think for a moment, and she gives me a tiny half-smile.

"Sometimes you're going to have to allow yourself to trust others if you want to get things done, Jack." I move into a crouch and offer her a hand. "C'mon. Let's get going. We all have a dinner to cook."

She doesn't take my hand, so I let her be alone for a minute. When she joins us all around the fire, she's quiet. I think about what might be bothering her but try to shake the thought away. My mind has already been clouded with Jack too much for today.

Jack

WE HAD DINNER ABOUT AN hour ago and the last rays of the sun are gone. I'm sitting here, watching the fire dance on orange coals with my insulated bottle of water in one hand. Of all times, why couldn't it simply turn into a glass of Chardonnay? Luca sits across the fire, holding his own in conversation with Derrick and Anthony. He's easy-going and a great fit in the boy's club, and that just chaps me in all the wrong places. Then again, there were the comments he made earlier about my talent and his advice about teamwork. Guess I'm learning a little about it myself out here.

Luca sips from his canteen. I grab mine too, wishing for a cup of *Hand of the King* tea from Dartealing Lounge.

The fire we sit around is small, but it's warm enough to keep the night chill away. The smell makes me feel more homesick than I would like to admit. It's a reminder of the wood-burning fireplace in my family's den on cool evenings. I grimace as I wonder what Mama would say about the mess I've created. I can almost hear her voice now.

You should think these things through, Jacqueline. Or: Haven't we taught you better than to go off on a whim like that? Or: You're always the one to jump into something before you know what the consequences are.

Geez. I've tried. I'm *always* trying. And trying is exhausting.

Regardless, it's too late now to avoid this situation. I need to just get through this week and back to where I'm comfortable. The next time Mari comes up with one of her harebrained schemes, I need to stay as far away from it as I possibly can.

"I think I've got a quarter in my pocket I could offer you for your thoughts." Emma takes a seat on the ground beside me. Our shoulders touch as if we were childhood friends.

"I'm pretty sure my thoughts aren't even worth a dime." My words come out a little drier than I intend.

She leans into me, nudging me as if I'm talking nonsense—another more than familiar gesture. "Try me. I'm a good listener."

My eyes betray me, flitting over to where Luca sits, but I catch myself and look directly at Emma. She hadn't missed a thing. At least she doesn't give me any grief about it. In fact, she has the sweetest smile with dimples in each cheek, and I can't help but have an immediate fondness for her. "Have you ever done something rash and immediately regretted it?"

She throws her head back and laughs once. Then, she sweeps her dark brown braid over one shoulder and pins me with a challenging stare. "I'd love for you to tell me one person who hasn't. In truth, I'd bet you a hundred bucks you can't."

I wave my hand in a wide motion around the fire. Slowly, though, so people don't get alerted. "Oh, all my coworkers. They seem to be pretty darn perfect. Self-assured. In the boardroom, out of the boardroom, putting up tents, riding horses. Heck, it doesn't really matter. They're all just *good* at it. And then look. Your husband melds right in, and so does he."

She furrows her brows. "Aren't you the one who organized this event?"

I heave a deep breath. "And therein lies my regret."

"You could have picked a retreat at a bed and breakfast or a five-star hotel in the city. Anything more upscale than this."

"You're right, I could have. But I was angry at the time. I was sick of being put into the girl's place at work, and my friend—bless her snarky little soul—got me to book it after a couple of drinks." I pick up a stick, start breaking pieces off, and throw them into the fire.

"So, before you booked it, what got your craw?"

"Huh?" I ask, wrinkling my nose.

"Sorry." Emma picks up another stick, starts peeling away the bark. "What were you upset about when you decided to book the cattle drive. Can I ask?"

"Oh." I scoff. "It's funny, really. Or not. I was upset about my boss asking me to coordinate the team outing. That's what I mean about the girl's stuff in the office. It seems so stereotypical that a *male* boss would ask his *female* employee to do all the planning work for the team fun."

"And what's so bad about doing that? Sounds kind of fun to me." She lifts a shoulder.

"I am not fun coordinator. It really doesn't come natural to me. And every time the boss needs something extra, or out of the office, planned, I'm the one that has to do it. They never ask Eddie or Nathan or Sean. It's always Jack." I lower my voice when my boss Geoffrey looks across the fire at me. "Or maybe it's 'Jack, can you take meeting notes?' As if I'm the team secretary."

"I see." Emma tosses a stick into the fire. I'll admit, I've never been in a corporate environment. I was born and raised here in New Mexico. A country girl. I went to college, but I didn't go for anything more than a business degree so that I could come back here and help with the ranch. Basic accounting, taxes, and such. And then I met Wyatt, and the rest is history."

She spreads her arms and looks up at the stars. "To me, there's not a better office on the planet. And I plan most of the 'fun,' I guess you'd call it, around the ranch."

I open my mouth and close it again. "That's different. You're *running* the business."

"Let me ask you this." She purses her lips and takes an audible breath. "Have you directly mentioned your frustration to your boss?"

Biting my lip, I let out a long exhale. "I haven't, but that's beside the point."

"Is it?"

It's a good question, but I don't feel like it's my place to correct everyone's view of women in LivFit. There's no purpose in harping on it, at least for tonight. Instead, I ask, "What about Luca? How did he end up here?"

"That, love, is not my story to tell, but he and Wyatt were college buddies. He joined us on the ranch about a year and a half ago. And I tell you what, he is a totally different person since he left Cali. He may have been well on his way to a heart attack before that." She tosses the last bit of her stick into the fire.

I swivel my head over to look at Emma. "He's from Cali?" He mentioned the city, but I assumed Albuquerque or maybe Denver.

"Yup." She glances at the man in question. "There's often a whole lot more under all the denim and the boots that you'll see out here in the desert. Don't be so quick to judge." She pats my knee and stands up. "I'm heading for bed. I suggest you go rest up too."

The others around us peel off and crawl into their tents, so I do the same. I take about twenty minutes to get comfortable enough to settle, and still, my mind races for a long time after. The voices around camp die down and the only sound is insects chirping in the night. It's disturbingly quiet, but it feels almost like the sounds they pipe in during the relaxation massage at the Golden Orchid spa down the street from my townhouse.

I take long and slow deep breaths, counting, and force my eyes to remain closed. Somehow the images that play across my mind as I'm feeling the pull into sleep are all of Luca. I drift off, wondering why I find myself so curious about this strange cowboy.

Chapter Six

I WAKE UP WITH A STICK in my back and a crick in my neck. It's not even daylight out, for goodness sake. But there is no way I'm going back to sleep on this hard ground. My mind races with all the things that we've got planned today or, at least, what I think we have planned. We're supposed to drive the cattle until lunch today and then stop for team building. Some calf tying, some horseshoes, and some other activities that are about the last things in the world I am looking forward to. The touchy-feely things aren't my cuppa tea. I'd much rather focus on getting the job done than feeling good about the team.

I slide into my boots and jeans and pull a T-shirt over my head.

Just as I'm about to stand, a cowbell rings.

Emma's voice follows. "Breakfast."

I duck through the tent flap and unfold myself to stand upright in the cool morning. As my fingers comb through my hair, I wish there was a hot shower nearby. Everybody else seems to gather around for breakfast. Wyatt passes out bowls and Emma stirs something in a steaming black pot.

Eddie grabs two bowls and brings one over to meet me halfway to the breakfast table. "How did you sleep?"

I grumble. It's hard to be enthusiastic this early in the morning, but somehow Eddie has the market on it. Don't get me wrong, I love him to death, but I just can't understand how chipper he is all the time. It's time for me to be that upbeat. After all, I have to assume the title of Fun Coordinator this afternoon. At least I'll have this morning's ride to give myself all the pep talks I'll need to bring my A-game. "Better than I expected," I answer with a forced smile. "Guess the riding yesterday did me in."

The sound of galloping grabs our attention, and we both turn in time to see Luca riding his mare up the hill. My cheeks go hot, and I inadvertently lift one hand to touch my face.

Before Luca can bring his mare to a stop, a hand waves back and forth in front of my eyes. I blink and look over at Eddie, who just chuckles.

"Let's get you some more oatmeal. It's going to be another long day."

"Yeah, absolutely. After breakfast, I need to find service and call Jane to check on the status of the project."

Eddie shoots me his best accusatory look. "You're

kidding, right? You said you were going to get all of that wrapped up before you left, so you would not worry about the project while you were out here."

The sad thing is, he's not wrong.

After I eat a bowl of pasty oatmeal, I run up the hill and take my phone out to get a signal. If I'm quick about it, I can check in and be back before anybody's ready to get on the trail for the day.

Luca

EMMA REACHES OUT WITH A stack of clean dishes to hold while she is packing things away. But as soon as I reach for them, there's a blood-curdling scream from over the hill. The dishes go clattering to the ground.

I sprint up the hill to find Jack, who is frozen with her hands in the air, phone in one hand, and both hands trembling. There's a four-foot-high boulder in front of her, and she's face to face with a snake sunning itself on top of the enormous rock. My hand drifts toward the gun holster, and I study the snake, also perking my ears to make sure it's not a rattler. It's quiet, and the alternating brown-and-cream colored bands give it away as a harmless kingsnake. The gun shouldn't be necessary. Although, even though their bite is harmless, they do bite, and that would put Jack over every edge that exists and ensure she would never come into the wilderness again.

"Jack, you're fine," I say, as I approach her slowly from behind, and brush my hand softly down her shoulder.

Jack sinks into me with the touch of my hand. I put

my mouth next to her ear and whisper, "You're okay. It's not a poisonous snake. Just back away slowly."

In my mind, I can picture the snake lunging at Jack out of fear. No one can forget a snake bite, even if it isn't poisonous. Jack keeps her hands extended in the air and moves to the side. The kingsnake tracks our movement and brings its body around—the beginning of coiling for a strike. I take my hand and put it in the curve between Jack's ribs and hipbone and move her behind me until it's me face to face with the snake.

We both back away, taking slow strides. Snakes aren't typically the aggressors in situations with larger animals, but this big guy feels threatened. And, regardless, I still make it a habit to never look away from a snake. When we get a good ten yards away, the snake lowers its head to the rock, its eyes and forked tongue no longer scenting or searching for us.

"Oh my gosh, oh my gosh, oh my gosh," Jack says, slinging her arms around me. "I almost died. That was so close."

I want to tell her that the snake was harmless and more scared than she was, but instead, my reflexes kick in and I wrap my arms around her lower back, giving her a squeeze. And it feels a heck of a lot better than I'd like to admit. I haven't held a woman close to me since—no, I'm not bringing those memories into the daylight. That's ancient history and not a situation I care to relive.

"Why didn't you kill the snake?" Jack says as she pulls away from me, but she doesn't extract herself from my hold and her hands linger on my shoulders.

The flippant question brings me back to reality, and

I release my arms from around her waist. "Why would I kill a snake that is completely harmless? Kingsnakes keep the mouse and prairie dog populations down, so they're really good to have around."

Jack's mouth opens as if she has words about to fall from her lips but then she shuts it again. We stare at each other, both with our hands on our hips. She tucks her lips between her teeth so I can barely see them, and I remember who I'm dealing with. Despite her senseless corporate ambition, Jack's a girly girl. Not to mention a city slicker. I wonder if she watched that movie before she came out to commune with nature. She doesn't appreciate the wide open or the fact that staying calm during this situation is the only thing that got her out of it safely—and kept the snake alive too—both of which make up the optimal outcome, in my book.

I suppose I was wrong when I thought she was coming around yesterday.

"I know you don't like me," Jack says out of nowhere, her eyes lowering, and she kicks a rock on the ground. A small cloud of dust poofs up from the ground and then she turns on her heels and starts walking back to camp.

I follow, skipping to catch up with her. "Jack," I say. "This has nothing to do with liking you or not. I don't kill animals for the sake of killing them. I assessed the risk and got you out of the situation."

"Fine," she puffs, never looking at me. "You saved me. Thank you."

"Fine," I repeat, furrowing my brows, because for the first time in my life outside of Corporate America, I don't want someone else to get the last word in.

When we reach camp, all eyes look at us, and Jack hurries over to pack up her tent and other belongings for the ride out. I stroll over to Wyatt, who looks at me for answers. I just shrug. I don't understand women and probably never will.

Jack

THE MORNING RIDE IS FAIRLY routine, if yesterday's ride was any indication. After packing up, we all humped our packs back to where we hobbled the horses and mounted up for the day. Luca and Wyatt opened the pen and the cows emerged without much prodding. We broke into our assigned groups and commenced the ride.

The group I was with took the left side of the herd with Frankie at our side. It seemed Butch was Wyatt's companion at the rear of the herd and Cassidy took his place with Emma on the right flank. The sun came up to our right but a little behind us, and I was grateful we were heading northwest to avoid having the morning glare directly in our eyes.

The morning passed with only a few words uttered to the backdrop of clomping, moos, and a bark punctuating the ride when one of the cows got out of line. My stomach rumbles a little by the time we approach a small grove of trees, and I'm sweating from the day's rising heat.

Luca points. "We'll rest there until this evening and then ride another hour or so to camp."

Breathe slowly, I tell myself. *It's only a few games. You'll do fine.* Even though I'm not keen on the team building that's about to ensue, it'll be good to be in the shade for lunch and the activities.

I stop Jasper next to Luca's horse and dismount, retrieving the small bag I brought with supplies for the games I have planned. The other two groups join us, and they slide down from their horses too.

"Do we need to hobble them again?" I ask Wyatt.

"Nah, they know the routine and we'll be right here near them," he answers.

Emma rides up last and leaps off her horse before he's even stopped. "Hey hon, help me with lunch?"

Wyatt tips his head to us and heads over to join his wife.

I walk into the copse of trees, searching the ground and every large rock. My hands shake a little as I remember the snake encounter. I'm not about to be that unobservant again, so I take several deep breaths to try to expend the adrenaline running through my veins. When I'm satisfied the area is clear, my heartbeat starts to settle. But then I pull a thin rope out of the bag, shiver, and immediately drop it because it reminds me of how the snake was coiled on that boulder.

Eddie, who's turning out to always be the trusty friend, jogs over and bends down to pick it up. Handing the rope back to me, he asks, "What was up with that scream this morning? And what's up with you . . . and Luca?" One of his brows quirk up suggestively.

"I was trying to find a signal to call LivFit and touch base with Jane about the project. I'm worried about quality assurance. So, I went up to the ridge and this ginormous snake came out of nowhere. I swear that thing was ten feet long. Are anacondas native to New Mexico?" I shudder again, remembering how it hissed as I reached out to lean on the boulder.

Eddie chuckles. "I don't think so. But rattlesnakes are."

I glower at him. "Not helpful in the slightest. Besides, Luca said it wasn't poisonous."

For some reason Eddie can't turn off his bright grin. "Wow. But everybody's okay, yeah? What did Luca do to take care of it?"

"Nothing," I answer bitterly, reach for the rope, and uncoil it. "The snake lost interest when Luca moved me away from the boulder."

"Moved you, huh?"

"Mm-hmm." I blink several times and shake my head. It was only my fear speaking when I asked him to kill the snake. It niggles under my skin that he was right, but I'm sure as heck glad he was. And then there was that hug. During the drive, I'd all but forgotten about the snake, but I couldn't banish the thought of Luca's arms around me. Jumping into him was a relief reaction on my part, but I can't regret it. The man's arms are so strong, and I'd be lying if I said I didn't enjoy the way he squeezed me around the waist. I glance over to where he's helping Emma and Wyatt.

"What's that smile?" Eddie asks.

Caught daydreaming about something I shouldn't, I sigh and refocus on my coworker. "Let's just get on with the games. Here." I hand one end of the rope to Eddie. "Tie this around that tree and I'll tie the other end around that one. About waist height."

He gives me a strange look but does what I ask. In my peripheral vision, the two cowboys have stopped unloading the picnic lunch supplies and stand like mirror images—booted feet shoulder width apart, arms crossed over their chests, and their hats pointed toward each other as they chat about something. Every few seconds, they glance over at our group, and a chill runs down my spine when Luca's dark eyes lock with mine. I look down quickly—caught staring—and finish knotting off the rope around the tree.

When the line is tied, I pluck it to make sure it's taut and wave everybody over. "This activity is called an electric fence. The object is . . ."

I take one look at Bruce, my peer who had hip surgery not too long ago, and I worry about his participation in this activity. I hold up my index finger. "Everybody, hold that thought. Bruce, can I talk to you over here?"

He limps over to the other side of the tree and stands in front of me, arms folded as he looks down. Even though we've been working at the same company for over a year, I didn't quite realize how tall and lanky this man was. Perhaps because there's rarely a need to get this close to him. I clear my throat and ask, "How's the hip?"

"It's holding up. The surrounding muscles are aching like there's no tomorrow, but it's solid. Doc did a fantastic job."

With a single nod, I decide I've made the right decision and continue. "I think you probably should play the role of leader on this one, given your recent surgery."

He scowls at me. "I'm riding a horse just fine. I think I'll be okay for one of your little *team building games*." He raises both eyebrows, bobbles his head on the last part, and takes a deep breath. "You don't need to mother me, Jack, especially since you're younger than my youngest child." He turns away from me to rejoin the team.

My blood boils for a hot second over the mothering comment, but I recover quickly. "You're right, but—" I grab his arm, and he stumbles as I pull him around. Case in point. Not that I would say that to him or wish hip replacement surgery on anyone. Still, it's a little nice to be right. "I know you signed a release, but this might require some awkward bending. I'd rather be safe than sorry." I pause to wait for him to give in, but there's very little except a stubborn set to his jaw. I try a different tactic. "Please?"

Bruce purses his lips but then nods. Good. "Your goal as the leader is to figure out how to get us over the rope without touching it. Caveat: we all must be touching one another throughout the activity. The object is to cross over the electric fence one at a time and not touch the electric fence. If anyone breaks the rules, you make us all start over. You can take suggestions from your team, but it's your final decision how we get over the rope. Easy enough?"

"As pie," he answers.

"I will facilitate a team discussion after the activity."

"Oh, boy. Maybe I'm happy to be leading this one." He rolls his eyes.

As we take the first steps on our return to the group, my eyes drift over to where Luca and Wyatt were standing. Wyatt's still there, but in the few seconds I spoke with Bruce, Luca has disappeared.

I stand next to Eddie as Bruce starts explaining the objective of this activity. I try to pay attention, but I'm keeping one eye out for Luca.

When Bruce finishes, Derrick pipes up, "Let's start by holding hands in a line. The tallest people can probably just step over the line."

I've done this activity before, and it's much trickier than that. But I keep my mouth shut, because I've seen some of the best ways to conquer the challenge. The first up is Sean, the tallest in the group, but as he tries to straddle it, the rope starts swinging.

Bruce calls out, "Nope! You just fried the whole team. Start over. Anyone have a different suggestion?"

As he's prompting the team, Luca reappears from over a small hill, leading a calf on a rope. The surrounding noise fades a little as I watch his slightly bow-legged walk.

Luca

As I return to the shady area with one of the calves that wouldn't leave the heifer alone, I can see a team-building game in full swing. There is a rope, and two of the men decided to get down on bended knee. I walk closer to the activity with the calf but stand back and see how everything will play out. I'm a little intrigued by the kindergarten-age nature of it.

"Jack, why don't you try to cross? You could put your

weight on my leg and then Calvin's to get over the rope," Sean says.

Jack smiles, like Sean has solved some sort of riddle that no one else is aware of.

"Let's try it," she says.

Jack puts her weight on Calvin first, and he wraps his hand around her waist to balance her. She then puts her foot down on Sean and steadies herself. She's not very tall, but she manages to hop over the rope, never letting go of Calvin's hand.

"That's one. Calvin, you have to come next," Jack says, continuing to look proud of herself.

I watch as one after another makes it over the rope. No one ever breaks the connection with the others. Sean comes last. Eddie, from the finished side of the rope, takes one knee to allow Sean a step. From there, the man is so tall, he clears the rope without much effort. The whole team stands and cheers.

Jack is a good teammate, I'm realizing. She doles out positive reinforcement and high tens to everyone on the team. Perhaps it's a show, but she sure seems like the biggest cheerleader of the group. It's high spirits all around. Even those who went into the activity skeptical of the thought of forced team fun is smiling now.

Jack's big brown eyes flit over to meet mine before she focuses on the team, and the question she asks is quite the surprise falling from her lips. "What exactly did we learn from this game about . . . trust?"

A smile spreads on my face as I turn and stroke the calf's neck. Perhaps this retreat is the perfect place for a girl named Jack after all.

Chapter Seven

Jack

A COWBELL CLANGS IN THE DISTANCE, and I look over to where Emma has a couple trays of sandwiches, bags of chips, and bottled waters lined up on a log she's using as a makeshift table. Wyatt, standing beside her, chews thoughtfully and laughs as she snuggles up to him to whisper something only for his ears. How adorable, I think as I avert my eyes.

The rest of my team starts veering in the direction of the food, but Eddie remains behind and starts untying the knot I made to secure the rope around the tree. I trail my hand along the braid to the other end to do the same. When I circle the trunk and reach for the knot, Luca's hand darts into my vision.

I gasp and look around to see the calf he was leading tied off to a stump.

Luca begins working at the knot, but his brow furrows

and he leans closer to examine my work. "Where'd you learn to make knots?"

"Well, not in Boy Scouts." I snort, thinking I'm making a joke. But then I realize it just comes off as awkward and I fight the urge to slap myself in the forehead with the heel of my hand.

Luca lifts one brow, but thankfully, he doesn't comment on my bad attempt at humor.

I tuck my hair behind my ear. "It's actually a surgical knot. My parents . . ." I suck in a breath and tuck my lips between my teeth. I don't need to share my whole life story with Luca, but somehow that little detail tumbled out without thought.

He makes an "ah" expression as if that cleared everything up. "I'm not sure you needed a triple square knot for this purpose."

As he works on removing my piece of work, I stand by and watch, not knowing what to do with myself or why he suddenly came over to help. I inhale and open my mouth to ask when Eddie comes around the other side of the tree. "Hey . . . uh, oh! Hi, Luca." He stops on Luca's other side and makes direct eye contact with me, wagging his brows.

I make the cut-off sigh, hand across my throat, fist it, and shove it back into my pocket when Luca glances over.

He finishes with the rope and holds it out to Eddie. "Wanna put that away for Jack?"

Eddie's shock turns into a devious smile. "Of course. I'll just . . . ah . . . leave you two kids to it." He winks at me and simultaneously hops and turns to jog in the other direction.

Luca leans a shoulder onto the tree and crosses his arms over his chest, facing me so that his broad shoulders block the view from everyone else. "So, games that reinforce trust, yeah?"

My cheeks flare. "It's just something I found online. These games are so cheesy." I roll my eyes and hold out a hand, trying to brush it off as total coincidence.

He purses his lips and nods musingly or perhaps accusingly. Or maybe a bit disbelievingly.

But my attention isn't on what's behind his expression, because my gaze has drifted down to his lips. For the first time, I notice how incredibly full they look and how . . . I blink and shake my head quickly. *What in the world are you thinking, Jack?*

"Well," he says, "I thought you did a wonderful job, wherever it came from. And you say your parents are surgeons?"

My eyes widen, and I stammer, "Uh, yeah." I haven't talked to anyone about my parents and their high-pressure expectations. Not even Mari. And I'm not about to get into that conversation out here with a near stranger. Although, he's not feeling like a stranger anymore, and I can't figure out why I want to be more open with him than anyone else. I fidget and take a few steps to move around him. "We, ah, should join the others for lunch."

I walk away, and after a few steps, his boots crunch in the gravely sand behind me. I stand near Emma, who looks up at Luca and clears her throat. With chagrin, he swipes a sandwich from her hand and turns away to retrieve the calf he left tied to the tree. As he's walking away, Emma hands me a napkin-wrapped sandwich. "Sorry. We don't have much out here except for cheese."

"No worries." I accept the offering and open it up just as Eddie comes over. I shove a huge bite of cheese and mayo sandwich into my mouth so I don't have to speak. He's smiling, and his little jibing is the last thing I want to deal with at the moment.

After lunch, we mount up and get back on the trail in the same formation; Wyatt's group to the right, Emma's to the rear, and us on the left. The drive into the afternoon goes smoothly and everyone is quiet. We'll apparently arrive in a couple of hours and Emma mentions a wagon will be waiting us there with more supplies for dinner. She'd sent someone to grab some things that would better fit my diet.

Suddenly, Wyatt whistles from across the herd and Frankie lets out a bark.

"Go on, girl," Luca says, and the dog runs back and around the rear toward Wyatt's side.

There's a dust cloud over there.

"What's happening?" I ask.

"A few cows probably got out of line, and Wyatt's working them back into the herd. Happens all the time," Luca answers.

Things settle down after the small excitement, and Luca turns Lucy away. "I'll be right back."

I watch him ride around and pull his horse up beside

Emma and chat for a second before continuing on to the far side of the herd. There's a hill we're cresting, so he ends up a little out of sight. I focus on the horizon where the cows are now descending into another valley. Hoof beats on the ground ahead stir up a bit more dust.

"Uh, Eddie?" I call over my shoulder.

He trots his horse alongside Jasper, eyes trained in the same direction.

I point. "Is there something we should do?"

"Ho-ly buckets," Eddie drawls. "Can you whistle like Wyatt did?"

"Are you kidding? I can barely make a sound when I try to whistle."

Behind us, Calvin curses.

The dust cloud gets bigger, so I call out. "Emma!"

I can barely see her from where we are, but she puts two fingers in the corners of her mouth and lets out a sharp sound of her own. A second later, Luca and Lucy appear at a full gallop, and his voice barks some commands as he leans forward into the gallop and passes Emma's group. Frankie, Butch, and Cassidy round the back of the herd first and pass us like the wind. Luca comes flying by next, and Jasper starts to stir beneath me. My heart echoes the hoofbeats and my hands start to shake, but I take a deep breath and pull back slightly on the reins, recalling how Luca taught me before. "Whoa. Steady. Whoa," I say, somehow keeping my voice super calm.

But I'm curious too, so I nudge Jasper forward. When

we crest the hill, the commotion becomes more apparent. A group of about a half-dozen cows have started to run toward a windmill off to the left, whereas the rest of the herd veers to the right.

The dogs work as a team on the left of the cows, turning their stampede, but the beastly cows are still in a good run. Butch nips at the front cow's leg just as the group reaches a small ridge, and the cattle begin running along the ridge.

I'm holding my breath as Luca and Lucy reach the ridge too. It seems like they've made the first turn successfully. Lucy leaps up onto the ridge and then rears up. Luca holds on, leaning forward while her front hooves kick into open air. It's a thing of beauty to watch, but I can't tell why she bucked. Something spooked her. It all seems to happen in slow motion and then she twists as she comes down and Luca tumbles from her back. Lucy runs straight back toward us.

My mouth is hanging, and instinctively, I urge Jasper into a run. When we reach Luca, he's just standing up and saying some not-so-nice things about that "wicked mare."

He dusts off his jeans and looks over at the still running cows. "Come-bye!" he calls, and the dogs repeat the maneuver to push the cows into a turn again. "Steady," he calls next, and Butch goes out front to slow the herd. They're heading back in the direction of the larger herd now, so it seems the catastrophe is avoided.

I pull Jasper to a stop near Luca and look down at him from my perch. It seems the roles are reversed now, and I smirk at him. But I can't hold in a laugh that comes bubbling up from my chest.

"Go ahead . . . laugh it up."

Luca

Jack is by my side before my ego has a chance to recover. I dig my fingers into my back, trying to detect any soreness from being bucked off of Lucy. But it seems my body is intact. Yep. Just my ego was hurt this time.

"I wish I had my phone out to record that," Jack says, jumping off of Jasper, keeled over laughing. "It was like it happened in slow motion. You falling backwards. Through the air. A look on your face."

I stare at Jack straight-faced as she continues to laugh. Me falling off a horse. The funniest thing she's ever seen. I whistle to Lucy, who comes trotting back to me. No longer spooked by whatever caused her to buck me off of her.

"I'm sorry," Jack says, finally composed. "It's just, well, you seem to do everything perfectly out here. I enjoyed the fact that you are, in fact, human."

The dogs follow us, surrounding the cows, who now come in our direction as well.

"You needed proof that I was human?" I look down at her as we both guide our horses by the reins.

Jack inhales sharply and then slowly lets her breath out. "I've been messing up since the day I arrived. That's all I'm saying."

My pride dissipates as I listen to Jack. Color

flushes her face and, in that moment, I stop taking myself so seriously. Had the roles been reversed, I would have laughed too. Once I knew she wasn't hurt.

"It probably was pretty funny," I say, giving her a side grin.

"The way your arms flailed as you fell through the air."

"Jack," I say, leaning into her. "The entire fall was probably less than five seconds, but I had no less than a thousand thoughts go through my head in that period of time."

Jack smiles, and I don't say much else. Sometimes I feel like when she looks at me she can read my mind. And I don't want her to know that all thousand thoughts that went through my head involved her.

Chapter Eight

Jack

MY STOMACH FEELS LIKE I did an intense ab workout yesterday but really, it hurts from all the laughing I did at the sight of Luca and the cows.

"How are you and the team holding up?" Wyatt asks me as his horse catches up to mine at the back of the line.

"No one will admit it, but I think everyone is finding something they enjoy from this retreat."

"That's great," Wyatt says. "I've been impressed with how everyone is stepping up in their own ways. Even you're starting to look like a real cowgirl, Jack."

"I've definitely tried to lean into this experience," I admit to Wyatt.

This entire retreat started as a joke. Or revenge against my team. But I've enjoyed sleeping under the stars. Getting my hands dirty. And doing things that I never imagined would be possible.

We all ride single file through the narrow clearing through the forest. It's beautiful; the way the sun escapes into small rays of light through the top of the trees. Frankie, the cattle dog, keeps all the cows in line, but members of LivFit contribute as well. I'm surprised at how much some of them have embraced this retreat. Especially Eddie. He's right up there, yelling at the cows and keeping them moving forward in somewhat of a straight line. That is no small feat. I wouldn't have pegged Eddie as someone who would step up and rise to the occasion.

The shade through the forest is a welcome change. Today is already gearing up to be a hot one, and the break from the sun is needed. When we get through the trees, the path widens, and Luca slows Lucy down to nearly a stop until our horses are next to each other.

"When's the next stop?" I ask Luca. One hand tightens on the rein and the other tucks a strand of hair behind my eyes.

"We're getting close. It's all downhill from here and then in another couple of miles, we'll reach a flat spot at the bottom of the hill, and that is where we'll call home for the evening."

I drop both reins to clap my hands together. Jasper looks up at me confused, but then I grip them once again.

"Good. I've got another fun game planned for when we stop," I say, unable to hide my excitement.

Luca rolls his eyes. He doesn't hide how he feels about these corporate retreat games.

"What's with you and all of these games?" he asks.

I smirk in Luca's direction. "I think you'll definitely want to participate in this one, Luca. You could use some practice in this area."

I laugh, as I bring Jasper to a gallop, and speed up ahead of Luca.

Luca

"Okay, the next event we're going to do is lasso the horse, but actually, it's just the tree stump over there. We're going to break into two teams, and once someone gets the rope around the stump, you have to race down, collect the rope, and pass it to the next teammate." Jack stands up tall as she explains the rules to everyone.

She glances in my direction, as I tie the calf to the tree. "Are you in, Luca?" I like how my name rolls off of her lips, and how she elongates the U in my name.

"I think I'll sit this one out and observe," I say, patting the calf on top of the head. Just wait until she sees what we have planned with the calf.

I think I see disappointment, but Jack stands next to Bruce, and they start counting teams into two. I've embarrassed myself enough for one trip. There's no way I want to botch the art of lassoing again.

The teams line up, and Jack once again glances in my direction. "Perhaps before we get started, we can have a real-life cowboy do a demonstration on how to properly lasso."

I roll my eyes and bark a laugh, but then I realize Jack is serious. She tosses me the rope, and I create a Honda knot, the kind I've tied a thousand of times before. Then, I take the second rope and do the same thing and toss them back in her direction. She is putting me on the spot. She wants me to fail.

But Jack lobs the rope back to me as if we were playing Hot Potato. She juts a hip and plants her fist on it. "We need a demonstration, cowboy." Jack winks at me, and if I'm not mistaken, she sounds a little flirty.

I hold the rope in my left hand and swing the other rope with my right. "Wyatt would be much better at this. He grew up doing it."

Wyatt smirks. "No way, *cowboy*, this is all you. Besides, I need to check in with Emma." He claps me on the shoulder as he effectively exits stage left.

"Alright, folks," I begin. "Let's forget about everything that happened yesterday so you can watch how to properly lasso a cow."

The group laughs, and I realize no one is making fun of me. Sometimes we hit the mark. Sometimes we don't.

"The important thing is after the release, follow through with your dominant hand."

I release the rope, and it sails through the air to land precisely with the stump at its center. I've roped cows from Jasper's back as they ran away, but I've never been this nervous doing such a simple act. All eyes are on me. Especially a pair of brown eyes that I'm desperate to forget but can't seem to stop thinking about.

The teams line up and they're ready to start. Jack does a count down, and when she yells go, the mood is frantic. The first two flail and end up with the ropes on the ground at their feet several times before they get it to rotate in the air. Even then, it takes them several tries to get one of the ropes to touch the stump. The mood is lively. Their skills leave a lot to be desired, but everyone is smiling and laughing, which is the entire point of this.

The first person finally finds success and runs the twenty-five yards to the tree stump, removes the rope, and sprints back to the team. The second team does the same, and the second players are up.

"Let's go, team," Jack yells. I never would have pegged her as a joiner, but she seems in her element.

When it's her time to go, I'm surprised at her lassoing technique. She isn't half bad. After about four tries, she gets the rope around the tree and sprints ahead.

"Keep going, Jack," her teammate, Eddie, yells. "You've got this. *Just like sweet-talking the water out of a well!*"

That one's a head scratcher, but the kid's on a roll with these quips.

The guy on the other team, whose name escapes me, sprints ahead to grab his rope from the stump. When he reaches it, he screams out, barrels toward the ground, and grabs his ankle with a huge groan.

"Nathan, are you okay?" The team rushes over to him, and I follow.

"Let's get his boot off," someone from the group shouts.

"No," Jack shouts. "The boot will help keep the swelling down until we can figure out what's going on."

Nathan rolls on the ground and moans once more. He's in a lot of pain.

"Emma!" I call, because I'm way out of my element when it comes to first aid.

Jack kneels beside Nathan and shoos everyone else back a couple of steps. "Take some deep breaths." She breathes along slowly as she reaches for his shoulder. Amazingly, Nathan begins following her instructions.

Emma runs over with the first aid kit, but it seems like she's a little too late to the party. Jack helps Nathan to reach a sitting position and then starts feeling around his ankle.

"Does it hurt when I press here?" she asks him.

Squatting beside the scene, Emma opens the kit.

Nathan winces but then answers, "No, the pain is lower." His voice doesn't sound like he's doing very well, and his face steadily drains of color.

Jack moves a finger to the tip of Nathan's boot toe and presses lightly. Her patient hisses in a breath through his teeth. Jack puffs her cheeks and blows out a steady stream of air as she shakes her head. She reaches into the first aid kit and brings out a wrap. "We need something more rigid to immobilize the ankle."

She looks up me. "Would you or someone else find some thin tree branches? I want to create a brace that will restrict movement." She glances at Nathan then, and her brows creep toward her hairline. "Heya, Eddie, can you grab me a blanket?"

Eddie skips into a run toward the horses.

I hesitate, surprised by Jack's confidence in what she's doing. I thought for sure Emma would need to jump in on this one. I point my thumb over my shoulder. "Yeah, I'll see what I can find."

But I can't seem to tear myself away from the scene, so I grab Sean's arm. "Would you mind finding a couple tree branches? Thin, but not too thin. Four or so?"

Jack has eased Nathan into a horizontal position by the time Eddie returns. "Under his head," she instructs him and calls after Sean, who's already heading toward the copse of trees, "Hey, Joe?"

He turns, and she continues, "Make sure they're around the same length." Then, to Eddie, she orders, "Keep him talking. Ask about his family or whatever."

Eddie follows her lead without question.

I crouch beside Jack.

She doesn't focus on my presence but continues working the scene while she narrates what needs to happen next. "I'm going to slide his boot off so I can get a better view of what we're dealing with here. I just need to see if anything's visibly broken and if he's getting blood to his toes and then we'll put it back on. That'll be the tougher part for him. Emma?"

"Yeah?" she answers without pause.

"Anything for pain in that thing?" Jack asks.

"Tylenol or Advil's the best we got."

"That'll do. Give him four if you have 'em. It'll help with the swelling and the pain." She pauses. "You know what . . . give him a couple of Tylenol too."

"What can I do?" I ask softly from beside her, but she doesn't answer immediately. She's too focused on the situation.

Jack is gentle in her touch as she unties Nathan's boot and slides it off of his foot. She presses on the outside of his ankle and the inside. She delicately moves his toes. All the things Emma would have done.

"I think it's just a sprain," she says, "but it'd be best if he had an X-Ray." She turns to me then, and her eyes have an intensity about them that's undeniable. She pauses, and her mouth works for a second before she finally asks me, "Any way we can get him to the hospital?"

"Ah, sure. I'll just . . . um . . . go and call for a ride." I stand.

"I've got it," Wyatt calls and turns for his horse.

And then I stand there, kicking myself for my thoughts and watching this amazing woman at work.

"Let's get your boot back on," she says to Nathan. "Good thing it ties. You've got a built-in compression wrap with that."

Nathan groans when she slides the boot back onto his foot and laces it pretty tight.

"Sorry," she says. "Just let me know if your toes start tingling."

"Very funny," he says through gritted teeth, and I can't help but snicker.

Sean returns with a handful of sticks and, with no help from anyone, Jack creates a brace that further limits his ankle movement. She flawlessly wraps the bandage around the twigs in figure eights, like she's done this a hundred times before. When it's done, she pats his knee. "Get it above your heart and keep it there, Nathan. It already bit swollen."

I pretend to wipe the dirt off of my jeans and continue to watch Jack as covertly as I can as she places a couple of bags under Nathan's ankle. It's easier for me to think of Jack as this prickly city slicker, who screams at the sight of harmless snakes and who cares more about the latest brand of leggings than for nature, but she continues to surprise me.

If I'm admitting it to myself, I found it quite attractive to watch her step up and help a teammate. She was in command, confident, calm, and nurturing. She wasn't nervous about breaking a nail or getting a little dirt on her fingers. I'm not wrong about most people, but maybe I had Jack pegged incorrectly.

She stands up once Nathan is situated and wipes the dirt off her leggings. She glances back at me, and this time, I don't even flinch when she catches me staring at her.

Yup. I'm in big trouble.

Chapter Nine

Jack

THIS MUST BE A COMMON stop along the cattle-drive route because there's windmill with a huge metal ring to collect the constant drizzle of water. A well powered by the wind, I assume. Emma filled up the water bladders she used to brew the coffee this morning and then took a handful straight from the pipe and drank. I grab my camp cup from Jasper and stroll over but far enough away to get some alone time and just breathe.

After Nathan's little incident—something I'll have to do a full write-up on for HR—I need to walk it off, and a glass of water sounds divine. Human resources, what another hassle. If only tending to peoples' health was all I had to do. There was a rush from being able to use those stale skills, and I can hear my father's voice in the back of my mind: *Why are you wasting away in the corporate world, Jacqueline? We put so much into your education, and you were on your way to being a talented doctor. The world needs more good doctors, you know.*

I take a long deep breath. I chose not to go into my family's preferred business for a good reason. I needed to make something my own, and I've been good at it too. So, why did using those stale skills feel so good?

We had planned to get back on the trail this afternoon and drive the cattle a few hours further toward the weekend destination, but I have no idea how long it'll take someone to get out here to drive Nathan back to town. It's entirely possible we will spend another night here before moving on. I'll have to ask Emma once she and a few of my colleagues have finished prepping lunch.

The metal ring is just a little higher than my knees, which makes it a little awkward to lean over. There's not a lot of water inside, just a little puddle maybe two feet in diameter. I plant one foot and lean toward the spout with my cup. Perhaps Dad was right and I'm wasting my career at LivFit. I'm definitely not using all the training I had before I took a left turn into the corporate life. The grass had seemed a bit greener over there with a nine to five job and not having to be on call. Although, I'm always on these days. And that's a little like being on call all the time. I take a deep breath and look up at the spinning blades as I wait for a small amount to drizzle in and pull it back to take a drink. It's ice cold and crisp on my tongue. With a sigh of refreshment, I smile and hold it under the stream to fill the cup.

Woof!

"Jack!"

I jump at the sudden, unexpected dog's bark and my name, and my balance falters. I reach for the spicket with my already outstretched hand. My cup goes tumbling into the muddy puddle, and the brown yuck is moving closer in slow motion when two hands land on either of my sides. The toe of one boot—Luca's well-worn boot— peeks at me for a split second before my body is rotated and I find myself looking up into his dark brown eyes with his arm cradling me over the puddle.

I'm not breathing.

Not moving.

What the heck am I supposed to do with this man so close? And so warm. Hot, even.

Under the shade offered by the brim of his hat, he smiles, and I think it's the first time I've seen a genuine smile on his face. "I gotcha."

I place both hands on his chest, hanging onto his shirt as if it was necessary to keep me out of the water. It's not, because his arm holds me effortlessly. My eyes drift down his nose to his lips, landing on the perfect cupid's bow on his upper lip. His lower lip is full too. . . Ah, no, that thought needs to stop right there. I finally inhale sharply through my nose and lean upward, trying to get him to stand me upright.

"Uhm, ah. Thanks," I stammer as he sets me on my feet, but he doesn't let go right away. I'm a bit overwhelmed by his strong arms, larger-than-life presence, and his scent enveloping me—leather and clean, but with an undertone of something slightly spicy. Perhaps nutmeg-ish?

Luca lifts a hand and sweeps a strand of hair away from my eyes, tucking it behind my ear. I feel his breath brush my temple and study his expression. It settles into a strange scowl, not a grumpy or angry one, but a confused look, as if he's confused but his interest is entirely piqued.

I lower my eyes, because I can't deny how good it feels to be standing this close to such a . . . yeah, I have to admit it . . . beautiful man.

"Yeah, sooo," I start, and at the same time, he says, "I just—" We both laugh quietly as we retreat from one another.

"Guess I'm not drinking out of that now." I step over the metal ring and bend to retrieve my now-muddy cup.

"Yeah, sorry about that. I didn't mean to scare you, but you must have been a million miles away to not have heard us running over." He jumps over the ring and crouches. "Here, let me grab that for you."

He rinses it off and holds it out to me, and I thank him.

The cattle dog hurtles the metal ring too, drops a ball at Luca's feet, and barks.

Luca picks it up. "All right, Frankie." He scratches the dog behind her black ear. The other is white, and she has one blue eye. Her entire body is giddy with anticipation as Luca rears back and launches the ball a good distance into the empty field. Frankie leaps from her still position over the ring and darts after it.

Luca sits on the ring, his boots crossed before him. He looks up at me with his hands shielding his eyes at the brim of his cowboy hat. "You were kind of spectacular back there while tending to Nathan's ankle. You seemed to know exactly what you were doing."

I sit next to him with my feet outside, watching Frankie as she runs a grid pattern in the distance searching for the ball. "I suppose that's thanks to growing up with doctor parents and having gone through a good deal of preparation for that career myself."

"Really? So, how did you end up working for a fitness device company?"

With both hands on the ring at my sides, I take a deep breath. Is this something I want to explain to a stranger? At length, I decide to keep it simple, factual. Vague. "I went to college to follow in their footsteps. Even got my BS in Bio-Sciences from Berkeley with a 3.9 GPA."

To his credit, Luca doesn't give me the standard brows-raised-and-lips-pursed nod. Instead, he waits patiently for me to continue.

I shrug one shoulder. "But I never really knew if that was me. So, after a year of medical school at UC San Fran, I changed directions and entered the MBA program."

He stares at me for several more minutes until the hairs on my arms stand up and I have the strange urge to cover myself. I raise a hand and rub the back of my neck, chuckling softly. "What? Not the story you expected? What about you?" I nudge him. "Emma said you lived in California, so what brought you all the way out here?"

Luca

THE QUESTION SHOULDN'T SURPRISE ME, but it does. I find myself wanting to hear more about Jack rather than talk about myself. Does she regret her decision to not study medicine? Is working at LivFit fulfilling? How does she handle the disappointment from her parents for not following in their footsteps? Or *are* they disappointed? Maybe not all parents are like mine over their children's choices to put aside a lucrative career. I take a deep breath to rid myself of that thought and size Jack up for a minute.

If there's anything I've learned, it's that getting to know someone involves reciprocation. I haven't always been good at that, but it seems I'm going to have to share too.

"I roomed with Wyatt at university."

"University?" Jack interrupts with a scoff. "I didn't have you as . . . ah, no matter." She waves a hand like she's waiving off the thought. "Where'd you go? Santa Barbara? Maybe, So Cal?"

I glance at her. Behind her kind eyes, there's what she thinks is a serious question. But those are party schools, and we were serious back then. Perhaps too serious. Despite her stereotyping, she seems to be genuinely curious.

She's also pretty smart and puts two and two together quickly. Her eyes widen when she obviously realizes what she's done. "Oh, I didn't mean any offense."

"None taken," I say, continuing to look at her. "Stanford. That's where I met Wyatt."

Jack removes her hand from her hips and pushes my shoulder playfully. "You went to Stanford?"

"Yeah. I studied software engineering and then

landed a job at Google. They put me through an additional two years of business school, and well, I worked for them for a few years afterward."

Jack doesn't hide her surprise. "That's a top-notch company, Luca. I've actually been eying a couple positions there in their wearable product development teams." She chews the inside of her lip for a moment and adds, "I'm still confused how you ended up here."

Jack leans in, although I don't understand why she's interested in my backstory. Her knee brushes up against mine, and I can't help but feel a jolt of electricity.

"I won't bore you the details," I say, "but I realized I wasn't cut out for the corporate world. Wyatt and I have been best friends since university and kept in touch. When he told me he and Emma were getting married and moving back to New Mexico and take over her family's business of ranching, I was floored. I visited every year, and it was the best week of that year. So, when he mentioned they needed help running the place, I jumped at the opportunity."

I decide to leave out some of the details. Like my five-year relationship with Viveka, who I worked with at Google and that couldn't make myself propose. I also don't tell Jack about the ultimatum Viveka gave me and how relieved I was to have the exit. I should never have wasted five years of anyone's life, but the fact that I couldn't get excited about our relationship niggled beneath my skin. Hopefully, Viveka doesn't see it as a waste. One of my ex-employees on the Software R&D team called and let me know she was getting married a few years ago, and that's the last I've heard of her. In truth, I'm happy she finally got what she wanted.

My parent's disappointment is also part of the story that I leave out. They couldn't believe I walked away from such a profitable career to join Wyatt and his bride in the middle of nowhere. I believe Dad's exact words were, "You're throwing your life away, son."

I suppose I had attained the greener grass in his mind, because he always told me turning wrenches wasn't a life at all. From what I remember about my parents, they never brought work into their house. Home was only about family, and that's the way it should be.

Luckily, my mom and dad's disappointment were short lived. My younger sister, Lettie, didn't let them stay disappointed for long. The first Christmas I was here, she convinced them to come stay with us for our first country holiday, and once they saw me in my element, they realized that I was meant to be here. Ever since, it's been only support from them.

Jack's dainty fingers splayed across my knee jolts me back to the present. We both turn our bodies towards each other, and her face goes from curious to sad. She pulls her knees into her chest and hugs them with her arms.

"Don't you ever regret it? I mean, after all of that schooling the stable salary. Or the city life, the amazing food and culture at your fingertips. How could you just walk away?"

Jack's questions are similar to the some of the ones my parents asked me, but they're also devoid of judgment and contempt. Instead, I feel like she truly wants to know these things. As if she wants to know me.

My lips turn up in a smile. "You'd think, right? But

no. I have zero regrets. Every day, I get to wake up on this beautiful ranch, surrounded by nature, with the mountains in the distance. I basically live with two of my favorite people in the world. I've met interesting people along the way, most of all, you, Jack."

"That's brave," Jack says, and her voice trails off. She almost looks sad as she looks down at her lap.

I crave her eyes and feel loss when she's no longer looking at me, so I put my hand underneath her chin and nudge her face up again. Her eyes blink and flick up. I study them closer than I ever have. They remind me of the color of chestnuts. Or maybe caramel. I lean in to study them closer, and then I catch myself when I realize Jack and I are nose to nose.

"I'm sorry," I begin to say, but Jack wraps her hand around the nape of my neck and closes the gap between us until her soft lips are on mine. I don't shut my eyes; I'm too shocked. But neither does Jack. And after tasting the softness of her lips, and staring into her eyes, I decide on honey. The taste of her, the color of her eyes. Honey.

On cue, Frankie runs up behind me and barks, and Jack and I both pull away from each other.

"I didn't—" Jack begins, but I wave her words away frantically.

"No, no, it was my fault. I . . ." My voice trails off. I'm not sure what I was even going to say. I am sorry if I went too far? But I'm not sorry I kissed Jack. Or did she kiss me? Does it matter?

Jack shoots up to a standing position, fingers rubbing her lips. I follow suit. She looks around, clearly worried about being seen, but the group is well off in the distance. "I'm sure no one was looking in our direction."

"We shouldn't have kissed," Jack says, shaking her head, as if she wants the memory of it gone.

Jack's right. I didn't even think I liked her. I mean, she seems to want the opposite of the life I'm trying to build here. She lives in San Francisco, the city I couldn't get away from fast enough. She's girly and has big corporate aspirations. We are literally polar opposites. But my heart sinks a bit at her words.

"You're right, and I'm sorry if I took advantage of you in any way."

"You didn't," she says quickly. "I don't think anyone saw us. We need to just forget it ever happened, and this goes without saying, but we should never speak about it again." Jack hurries off. She practically runs back to the group.

I sit back down, and Frankie sits next to me. "Well, boy," I say. "I suppose I should thank you for bringing us back to reality."

My voice tries to deceive my heart, but I can't be sure it works. There's a depth to Jack, and well, I'd have to be blind not to admit how gorgeous she is. Frankie licks my hand, and I pat him on his head, and then stand up.

"Frankie, if you know what's good for you, keep me away from that woman."

We start back toward the group. I step slowly around the sagebrush and toss the ball. Frankie barks, runs to retrieve it, and then trots along beside me as we rejoin the group.

Jack

TRYING NOT TO TWITCH OVER how thrilling that little kiss was, I march back to camp. My cheeks are on fire and my heart thunders in my chest, so I take long, measured breaths to get myself under control. I keep my eyes trained on the ground, not wanting to trip over any stray rocks or critters. But in truth, that's a lie, I just don't want to face anyone at the moment.

"Really, Jack. What got into you?" I mumble to myself.

My lips still tingle, and the kiss was really . . . nice. There wasn't any real pressure behind it, and the way we just looked into each others' eyes, I think we were both stunned by how suddenly I grabbed Luca and pressed my mouth to his. It's awful that I made him feel the need to apologize, but I couldn't find any words to explain what I'd done. Heck, I didn't even understand why the conversation about him deciding to leave California drew me to him so much.

What I said, though, was right. No more thinking about it. Absolutely not. It's only the end of day two, so I have another three days to get through on this little outing with him so close everywhere I turn. Once I get back to San Fran, my head should clear a little. All this so-called fresh air is apparently impeding my judgment.

When I get back to the camp area, most of the team is pitching tents for the night. That much makes sense, because we still have to wait for transport to take Nathan to the nearest town. When I walk around the end of the wagon, I almost run into Eddie and Derrick, who load up one of the tents with the food and supplies from the wagon Emma has been driving. The tarp that normally covers it is off sits inside along with Nathan sits inside with his leg propped up.

Wyatt and Geoffrey return to grab one last crate that sits on the rear end of the wagon.

"What's this?" I ask Wyatt.

He and Geoffrey bend over and grab the crate at the same time, and there's a shared grunt as they stand. Wyatt says with a strain, "Emma can fill you in," and they march toward the tent.

But Emma is nowhere in sight. I climb into the wagon to check on Nathan, who's holding a canteen. He hisses when I touch the toe of his boot.

"Sorry," I look up into his now-glassy eyes and scowl. The pain must be sending him into a numb state.

"Ah. Bruce had some whiskey. 'S keeping the pain at bay for the most part." He lifts one shoulder, and I worry for a second he might toss himself off the bench.

I cross my arms over my chest. Figures that Bruce, of all the team members, would have brought something along. "Give me that." I dump it over the side of the wagon. "This'll be a real problem if they have to give you anything for the pain."

Nathan reaches for it, missing by almost a foot.

I set him back upright, take a long deep breath, and puff my cheeks as I exhale. Taking a seat on the facing bench, I ask, "Why are you in the wagon?"

"Ah, well, the transport to town can't make it out

here."

"Hey, Jack!" Emma says from behind me, and I turn. She gives me a sweet smile. "The horses are rested well enough, so I'm carrying him back to the ranch this evening. A driver will meet us there. There's a shorter route than we took yesterday, so I'll be there, have a good night's sleep, and return before mid-morning."

"What she said." Nathan grabs the now empty canteen and pouts.

"Can I get a bottle of water over here? In fact, make it two."

Emma hands me two bottles and shoots me a "he's-a-handful" smile. I wash out his water bottle, fill it up, and hand it back to him. "No more alcohol. If they have to take you into surgery, you'll have to sober up first. And that might mean rebreaking your bones so they can set them right." I stand and shuffle my way to the end of the wagon.

Wyatt returns with my boss at his side and offers a hand to help me jump down.

Geoffrey looks at me and says, "Jack, we're going to need someone to fill in for Emma tonight and cook dinner."

I open my mouth to object, but he's already turned away. I'm not a cook. In fact, I can burn a good pot of boiling water any day of the week, but that's not what keeps my mouth hanging open. It's delayed, but the gender bias of his words slaps me across the face again. My mouth gapes for several seconds, and then something brushes against my leg. I look down at the bushy tail on the ground and the black and white face with one blue eye staring up at me.

"What makes you think Jack is the best one to cook?" It's Luca's voice, and it's got a touch of anger inside that makes my mouth go dry.

I glance over to where he's standing with one hand on the wagon and another on his hip. His expression doesn't look any happier than mine, and at least he's saying something about it. I think it might be the first time I've heard a guy speak up in defense of a random sexist remark.

Geoffrey looks at him like it's the most insane question.

Luca shakes his head and scoffs at my boss. "Typical," he barks. "Part of why I left." He reaches for my elbow and turns me away. "C'mon Jack. I'll make dinner, but maybe you can assist."

Luca

MY GOAL WAS TO IGNORE Jack. To take a moment to myself and not think about the way her lips felt on mine. I planned to think of something else. Anything—no, *everything* else. But not about Jack's lips. Or eyes. Or. . . well, any part of her. But then Geoffrey had to go and say something stupid, and I couldn't keep my mouth shut.

I pull the food out of the cooler and lay out the tinfoil.

"Vegan, just for you," I say, without looking at Jack. Even though I don't glance up, her presence is everywhere.

Her scent. The way she breathes, the sound of the dirt as she kicks her boot up.

"I'm not vegan, only pescatarian." Jack sits on the log stoop and grabs a can opener for the beans. She doesn't say anything more, and I don't respond either. The silence lingers and thickens the air between us.

When the can is fully open, she holds it between her finger, and then sighs. "Thanks, Luca. For jumping in back there."

"Can't really imagine what it's like, being a woman and working for a guy like Geoffrey, I'll be honest," I say, spreading the tortilla chips onto the tinfoil, and then taking a spoonful of beans from the can Jack still holds. A bit of guilt niggles under my skin because I've seen it before. I just never did anything about it. Guess there's a first for everything.

"Can't say I really *like* working for a guy like Geoffrey," Jack says, this time turning her body toward me. "But believe it or not, there are bosses ten times worse than him. With Geoffrey, I know exactly what I'm getting, and I can navigate it. With others, it was like playing a game of chess every day."

Jack reaches into the cooler, grabs a bag of shredded cheese, and starts sprinkling it over the food. Chicken and black bean nachos over the fire, sans the chicken, is one of my favorite campfire meals. And one of the easiest. We sit side by side, effortlessly putting the food together, and then close up the tinfoil to heat over the fire.

Jack reaches into her boot and pulls out a flask.

"Shh," she says. "I may have stolen Bruce's whiskey."

Our eyes meet as she holds the flask to her lips and grins.

I never drink on the job, but one swig won't hurt, and I am dying to place my lips where Jack's have just been. I take a drink, and the liquid instantly warms my belly.

"Believe it or not," I say, "I've worked for guys like Geoffrey. Worse, even. I don't think I ever had a full appreciation for what the ladies in the office must have been feeling." I cough deliberately to keep myself from saying the next words on the tip of my tongue—*and you're the first woman I've been compelled to stand up for*. Instead, I find something less gushy to say. "I wish I could go back and be a better colleague."

Jack's eyes dart up at me. She seems surprised. It's clear we've both misunderstood each other. Jack is definitely not shallow. And I can't be sure what she thought of me, but it wasn't good.

"You're not the worst human in the world after all," Jack says, but then playfully nudges me in the shoulder.

"And you're not the uptight city slicker I once pegged you for," I say. "I mean look at you. You're cooking with me and haven't complained once."

This time, I nudge Jack in the shoulder as I take the last of the foil packets off the fire. I smile and look through the fire to find every one of her coworkers looking back at us. Most disapprovingly.

"Alright, everyone," I say, avoiding eye contact. "Soup's on."

After dinner and clean up, the mood feels heavy with Emma gone. I lay in my tent, fluff my pillow up under my head, and fold my arms underneath me. I look up through the unzipped skylight on my tent and feel like I can see the entire milky way. One of the reasons I chose this life over "success" at Google. Clean air and clear skies. Quiet nights where it's easy to pick out the big dipper. There's the little dipper and Mars glowing brightly.

A branch cracks outside of my tent, and I dart upright, but stay quiet. Then, another branch. And another. Finally, I hear a giggle off in the distance and my tent shakes.

"Game time!" a male voice calls out. "Starting now!"

I haven't played nighttime camping games since growing up in the bay area where all the neighborhood kids would meet up in my friend's backyard at dusk. We always played late into the evening, or until our parents called us home. The nostalgia overwhelms me and I reach for my boots. Then, I'm outside before anyone has to ask me twice.

Chapter Ten

Jack

I SHOOT UPRIGHT ON THE HARD sleeping pad, thankful for the sudden distraction from trying to force myself into sleep. Whatever this "game time" is Calvin calls for outside is going to save me from hours of mental toil—and perhaps a little physical angst too. I was trying to hold my eyes closed as I ran through counting sheep, deep breathing exercises, and the words my yoga practice leader used during savasana at the end of class. Yet the notion of sleep eluded me while my mind raced over that scorching kiss with Luca. I don't think I've ever felt a kiss all the way to my toes before, and how could one kiss feel so utterly . . . right. I guess there's a first for everything.

Outside, the moon is nearly full, and the stars are so much brighter than they ever are in the city. There's usually a golden haze over San Francisco, and the bay area is often blanketed in fog. This fresh air and clear night aren't things I've had much experience with, but somehow, it seems like the open night sinks into my pores, energizes my muscles, and strengthens my bones. This trip wasn't what I expected, but I'm finding a sense of peace and solitude out here I didn't expect.

Calvin waves everyone over like he's coordinating a sports team, as if it was what he was born to be a coach. I've often sensed that he's a little regretful that he doesn't have children who are interested in sports; not that it stops him from giving his dancer daughters a-hundred-and-ten percent of his attention. In fact, he leaves work at ten before four every day of the week so he can get them to practice. And he and his wife are adorably in love. I don't think I've seen them once when they weren't holding hands or displaying affection in some way.

I've always stayed away from that kind of thing, thinking it would hold me back. But I wonder . . . would that be so bad?

I brush both hands through my hair and put all my random thoughts away as Calvin says, "Gather up!"

The LivFit team falls eagerly into place. They're sporty people after all, and the camaraderie almost buzzes in the air. I glance to where the horses are hobbled at the same time Luca emerges from his tent with a huge smile on his face. He seems eager too. Apparently, everyone needs a little distraction from the excitement of the day. Nathan getting injured, Wyatt and Emma leaving . . . both events itch under everyone's skin, but I do wonder if the memory of our kiss is needling at Luca like it is with me.

Turning toward the fire where the others are gathered, I fold my arms and join them.

Eddie is stoking the fire while we move closer.

"So, is Sardines okay?" Calvin pauses, waiting for an answer. "Anyone played before?"

I've never heard of it, but it sounds uncomfortable. "Do we have to squeeze into something?" I ask, and the team chuckles.

Calvin doesn't answer immediately, so Bruce jumps in. "We're *not* squeezing together, are we?"

"Weeeellll, you could," says our self-nominated coach. "But only if someone picks a tight spot to hide."

Eddie stands up from the fire and gives Bruce a playful nudge. "Sounds like the key is to hide in plain sight."

Bruce gives a harumph and unscrews the cap on his flask, tossing it back, and then lets out a sigh. "I think I'm going to sit this one out."

"Suit yourself," says Calvin. "The game is really just hide and seek in reverse. Someone hides and everyone counts to . . . let's say a hundred, since there's so much open space here. When you reach a hundred, you start looking for the hider. If you find them, you stay there too, and so on until everyone finds the group."

Luca has arrived at my side and butts in. "And the last person who finds the hiding spot is the hider in the next round."

I look up at him, and words come tumbling out of my mouth. "Is this you volunteering to hide first?"

He shrugs and cocks a half-smile. "Sure. I'm game."

Luca

I HAVEN'T PLAYED SARDINES SINCE I was young. The neighborhood kids and I would play it at dusk for hours into the night until our parents called us in one-by-one. After the group dwindled to four or five, it wasn't a lot of fun anymore, so those of us remaining would head home for the evening. My parents were never too concerned, so I was always among the last of the group and the last one home since my house was at the very end of the cul-de-sac.

I glance back at the group. Calvin put on some music—some stereotypical country ballad from the 90s—but it helped cover the sound of my footsteps moving away from the group. Everyone near the fire has their eyes covered, and they're counting out loud in unison. Funny how that always happens. Usually, there's one person who starts out faster, but I think it's human nature to fall into a chorus.

I walk maybe a hundred paces eastward and turn to my left. It seems like I'm far enough away for it to take them some time to find me, but not so far that they'll be looking for more than fifteen minutes or so. I hide between two mountain mahoganies, which are everywhere on this part of the trail. The moon is the only thing that lights a path. It's dark and the shadows are deep.

The voices finish, and footsteps go off in every direction but no one says much. It's kind of fun to see a bunch of grown-up corporate folks playing a child's game, but it makes them a little more likable, in my book. I keep my breathing quiet as my eyes adjust to the darker area off-trail. A silhouette nears me, one I'm becoming quite familiar with. Jack tiptoes down the trail, clearly trying to make very little noise to tip her hand. She doesn't see me behind the bushes and starts to walk on by.

Quickly, I glance toward the fire and take note of where most of the team went. Then, my arm instinctively reaches out to her, I grasp her by the wrist, and pull her to me. She lets out an almost silent gasp, and I cover her mouth with my hand. When she understands it's me, I remove my hand.

Jack melts into me, her warm breath on my ear. "I don't think you get the concept of the game, Luca. I was supposed to find you. You weren't supposed to out yourself."

"You're wrong," I whisper. "I understand exactly what I'm doing."

Jack smiles up at me, and I pull her close to me as footsteps get closer, and then fade again. The space between the two bushes is narrow, so I wrap my arms more tightly around her. Jack leans into me and her arms settle around my waist.

Her body pressed against mine makes me hope the rest of LivFit never finds us. Because holding Jack under the moonlight is the best thing I've done in a long time.

"Luca," Jack says softly, I can feel the vibration of her voice against my chest.

I look down at her as her eyes search mine in the darkness. I take her chin in my hand.

"Luca," she says again. This time there's a note of

desire in it that stirs me in the heart. Such an emphasis on the u in my name, and the way her lips pout when she says my name makes me want to capture her bottom lip between my teeth. Our connection, surprising though it may be, is something I've never had before. I want to drink it in with every inch of my being, to drink *her* in and make this night go on forever.

I manage to pull her even closer. The moonlight shines on her hair and glints in her eyes. She licks her bottom lip—an invitation—and my lips once again find hers. This time, the kiss feels more meaningful, perhaps an answer to an unspoken expectation. But I quickly get out of my head and enjoy what she offers me.

Jack

WHAT AM I DOING?

No really. *What* am I doing?

Luca's lips are soft and demanding, and I'm happy to give them everything they ask for. There's this smell about him that's leathery, warm, and spicy—all man with a bit of rich, Italian seasoning. He tastes like that too—as if I'm in an old-fashioned home in southern Italy devouring a robustly sauced pasta. My hunger for this man makes it seem like I haven't eaten for days.

How does he do this to me? Every last kiss I've ever experienced before this made me question if I needed to kiss a man. In fact, I've often wondered if a woman would be a better choice. But this... I don't even know how to describe it. It's as if his presence is everywhere. All around me and possibly creeping inside.

My gut clenches. I move my hands up his torso, over his shoulders, and around his neck. A small sound escapes my throat, and he pulls back a little, smiling into my lips while keeping our foreheads pressed together.

I'm breathless, and if his arms around me let go, I'm not sure I can stand for how jelly-like the muscles in my legs feel. He kisses me again, softly, and then trails fluttery kisses down my chin and neck.

"Luca," I whisper, and he kisses back up my neck to my ear. "Should we be . . ."

I inhale and bite my bottom lip as his teeth graze my earlobe. Chills run down my spine, all the way to my toes.

His breath is hot in my ear when he asks simply, "Why shouldn't we be?"

I thread my fingers in his wavy hair, pull his lips back to mine and proceed to kiss him thoroughly. Our lips dance. I'm high or am I falling? Lost or found? Confused but oh so sure this is right.

I'm on the very tips of my toes, kissing him for all I'm worth, ready to wrap myself around Luca. And then, a throat clears dramatically behind me.

We stop mid-kiss. Simply halt. Luca and I don't move away from one another, but our eyes fly open and lock with each other's. Caught.

And then Eddie drawls in his mock-southern accented voice I'm certain everyone can hear it for miles around. "Well, well, well, *butter my butt and call me a biscuit!*"

Chapter Eleven

Howling comes from far in the distance through the thin tent walls. The coyotes must be gathering in the foothills, which means dawn must be near. I pull the pillow over my face and squeeze it to my ears. My body is heavy after running around for half the night, but the best part was catching Jack around the waist. My lips tingle with the memory of Jack's soft lips on mine, and my mouth waters over how sweet her kiss tasted.

But today is the last full day with this group and then she'll be heading back to California. That life almost killed me once. High blood pressure, high cholesterol, prediabetes. Yeah, all that was attributable to sitting behind a desk or in a conference room for ninety percent of my day and breathing smog when I wasn't letting my rear-end get numb in an office chair. Stupid of me to let my health slide so much by the time I was thirty.

No. I won't go back to that hustle and bustle.

And, if I'm being real with myself, I'm way too old for her. She's probably not more than twenty-five. She's one of those people who find success through sheer determination and putting on the right persona at the right time. Okay, maybe she's twenty-six or -seven. Still, that's about twelve years younger than me.

I can't continue thinking of Jack with every waking—or half-waking—moment. Her place is climbing that ladder, at least for now. While we haven't discussed it at all, she's gotta be at least ten years younger than me. Perhaps she still has the energy to deal with that rat race. Heck, I have the energy now that I've gotten back in shape, but the desire to live that life? Nah, not really.

The howling sounds again, and I squeeze the pillow again along with my eyes. One more hour of sleep would be heaven at the moment before I have to get up and prep breakfast for this group.

A gunshot rings out in the next moment, and I dash up from my mat, grab my rifle, and am out of the tent in seconds. I squint and throw my arm up against the morning sun. It's later than I imagined; I never sleep past sunup. No one out here has guns out here except Wyatt and me, but he left yesterday with Emma.

My eyes flutter as I step out of my tent, blinking against the stinging, until the scene around me comes into focus. The entire group from LivFit is huddled together, eyes wide, near the stack of cooking supplies.

"Where'd the shot come from?" I ask. I was too disoriented to judge a direction while lying in my tent.

In unison, Eddie and Jack both point off in the direction of the herd and horses. Oh no. That's not good at all.

I drag a hand through my hair and duck back into my tent to put on my boots. There shouldn't be anybody out there, so I have to go check it out. I put my hat on and leave my tent flap wide open as I march outside. "You guys keep rolling with breakfast and I'll be back shortly." I skip into a jog as I pass them and make my way toward the horses we keep near camp.

"Luca!" Jack's voice calls after me.

I wave her off. "Everything will be fine. Take care of breakfast and I'll be right back."

I pass Lucy. She's a good horse, but Jasper is faster. I release his hobble, tie the rifle to his saddle, and hop up. When I dig my heels onto his sides, he takes off like lightning toward the herd. The cows aren't far, and it doesn't look like anything is amiss from this distance, but I still think it's strange that they haven't stirred with the gunshot.

I narrow my eyes toward the horses are on the far side of the cows and see Wyatt's paint stallion, Pirate, on the far side. Two black and white dogs are running about, keeping the herd steady.

Butch and Cassidy.

The knot in my stomach loosens, and I pull on Jasper's reins to slow him to a trot. A little pressure on my left knee signals him to circle the herd and aim for the mostly white horse with a dark-chocolate patch covering one eye; the reason Pirate got his name. As Jasper slows his gallop toward Pirate, I see a figure off in the distance. His cowboy hat is tipped down, but it is unmistakably

Wyatt with his pigeon-toed swagger. We never went unnoticed in college because his walk always screamed cowboy. Although, I've been developing that walk too with all the horseback riding. I wonder if I'd get the looks he used to get if I went back to the city.

There I go again, thinking about that life. It's not happening. Can't. Focus, Luca.

When Jasper halts, I stand in the stirrup and dismount. The horse is barely even breathing heavily, not that it was a long run. I stroke Jasper's neck for a second and coo, "Good boy. You wait here." Then, I turn toward Wyatt and start walking.

After about a dozen steps, Wyatt looks up. "Mornin'." He waves with his rifle hand.

"What's going on? I didn't expect you to be back so early." I pause and turn as he meets me, and we walk casually, together, back toward the horses.

"Coyotes were circling. Got one before the rest went running for the hills. Plus, I really didn't want to leave you with the crew alone."

"Is Emma on her way back too?"

"She's waiting to meet the transport, and then she'll head back to meet us with the wagon. I doubt she'll make it before supper time."

I slide my hat from my head and scratch behind my ear. "So, we're waiting another day before we head out? Won't that put the LivFit team off their flight schedules?"

"Nah. We'll leave today. We should be able to get most of the supplies onto the horses and make it to the next stop. I called Sid to let him know we were running a little behind. We need to try to make up time so the team can catch their flights out of Albuquerque."

"Good idea." I slide my hat back on and look off into the foothills away from Wyatt. Why is it that something inside makes me not want this week to end? "But do you really think that's wise? I mean, we've already had one person hurt. What about that guy with a bad hip? What was his name?"

Wyatt stops, his footsteps no longer kicking up sand beside me, so I turn to find him staring at me with narrowed eyes.

"What?" I ask.

"Something's wrong? You're different. What happened while I was gone?"

I am not about to tell him that Jack is drawing me in like a fish on a line. And that kiss was sure as heck none of his business. "Nothing. I'm just worried that it'll draw another insurance claim if we have anybody else hurt," I lie.

"Hmm," he mumbles. "Sure does feel like you're dancing around something else. Doesn't have to do with—"

"No!" I snap, then continue in a more controlled tone, "No. I'm as anxious to get on the trail as you." I tip my head toward the horses. "Let's go see what Bruce thinks. That's the hip-guy's name."

"Maybe we should ask Jack. She's the coordinator and seems like the one who'd be in charge of their workman's comp issues."

"Uh, yeah. Ah . . ." I pick up the pace. "Why don't you, um, do that?"

Jack

MY PEERS DECIDE LUCA HAS things under control and work to put breakfast together, but I'm watching, pacing, and biting at my thumbnail as if that'll help the situation. Sean and Calvin have the cooking portion in-hand. Meanwhile, I stop my pacing on a spot facing the herd, shoulder-to-shoulder with Eddie. I wait to find out what the disturbance was, when Luca and Jasper ride back to the camp. Wyatt and his mostly white stallion trail Luca by two horse-lengths.

Luca stands in the stirrups, throws his leg over, and walks alongside Jasper in the blink of an eye. His jaw is set in a way I don't think I've seen yet. Determination, perhaps, and he marches directly for me. I stand a little straighter, eyes wide. And when he reaches me, Luca shoves Jasper's reins in my hand without preamble then marches past me without a good morning or a hint of eye-contact.

I twirl on my heel and stare after him. His head hangs, shoulders hunch, so something has happened between last night and this morning. He makes for the supplies not being used for breakfast and starts trying to consolidate containers.

Eddie leans closer, his voice low. "Apparently that kiss last night *musta been nothin' to write home about.*"

I roll my eyes at his obsession with using southern phrases. I should have thrown that book he brought in the trash back at the airport. He's wrong, though. The kiss was everything to write home about, and I have the feeling Luca thinks so too. I'm bent on finding out what happened out there, for one, but also why Luca is being so cold after our connection yesterday. I hand the reins to Eddie and march over to Luca.

Slowing on my final few steps, I shove my hands into my blue-jeans pockets and try to seem sweet. Whatever the problem is, I doubt being direct—which is normally my M.O.—will calm him much. "Heya, cowboy," I say.

Luca doesn't look at me. Instead, he shoves a bag of gear into my arms. "Load this up onto Lucy's saddle." Then, he returns to consolidating the rest of the gear.

I hug the bag to my chest and dig in my heels. My mind spins, switching between anger and shock, but I'm not letting him get away with whatever this mercurial attitude is. Last night's connection was too much for me to just let it be. I drop the bag, sand billowing up around where it thuds to the ground, and plant both fists on my hips. "No."

A couple of the guys have started to stare at us, but I ignore them and wait. Finally, Luca stops his obsessive packing, stands straighter, and turns to face me. His mouth is formed, ready to ask one of the four Ws, but I hold my hand up, palm facing him.

My lips are pressed tightly, and I give the team watching us a leave-us-alone glare. Luca scowls at me expectantly as I gather my composure and say at last, "Over there." I march toward a tree some distance away from the others.

Behind me, I hear another of Eddie's newly learned

quips. *"Dang, she seems madder than a wet hen."*

Ignore it, I tell myself and march straight for somewhere that might give us just a little seclusion. Gravel crunches behind me, and when I reach the far side of the tree, I whirl around to face Luca. "What gives?"

He shrugs with both arms out, palms up. "I'm sorry, but I don't follow."

How can he sound so innocent? So aloof? So ignorant?

The howling and gunshot before fade into the background of my mind, only seeming to reflect whatever's happening between Luca and me. I glance back at the crew, where Wyatt has fallen into the breakfast routine. He seems A-okay, as if the morning's a hundred and ten percent routine, but there's something far out of sorts with Luca. Different even from before our connection.

I fold my arms over my chest. "Was our little make-out session last night something you do with a girl on the trail every trip? Then, just pretend it never happened? Really?"

He swipes off his hat and runs his hand over his head, sighing. "Jack, . . ." he says as if it's about to be followed by a blah-blah-*but* statement.

"Oh no, you don't!" I wag my finger in the air in a no-no gesture. "Uh-uh."

Luca takes a deep breath but doesn't offer an argument or explanation.

"Is it a standard thing for you? Is this really why you came out here to New Mexico from Cali? It wasn't for the wide open, was it? No, this ranch gives you the perfect opportunity to have a little fling with lonely girls who venture out on this—this. . ." I have to stop because my throat suddenly feels like it's closing. Lonely? Is that true for me? I spin around to hide my sudden emotion.

What in the world am I thinking? I'm reacting irrationally. He didn't give me cause to become all dramatic. This is insane! It was, like, two whole kisses, not as if we have a relationship or anything. Geez. Maybe I'm PMSing. I blink my eyes several times to extinguish the burning sensation and take a long, slow inhale. And another. Then, strong hands clasp gently onto both my shoulders. Luca turns me and pulls me into his arms. My body goes rigid, but at the same time, my heart sings.

"It's not like that, Jack," Luca says into my hair. "I haven't kissed anyone other than you in a very, very long time."

I stare at his hat on the ground for a few seconds and pull away a little to look up at him. The sun is behind his head and blinding, but he turns us so I don't have to squint. Such a little thing but, man, does it show how considerate he is.

"Is that so?" My voice is thin but hopeful, and I feel the corners of my lips turning upward.

"Yeah." He chuckles, the power of his voice radiating through his chest and into me. "I haven't kissed anyone in probably eight years. Dang, make that nine. Not since I broke it off with my ex-fiancé and moved out here."

My eyes stretch. "You were engaged?"

He laughs again. "I was. I met Sonja in college." He

presses his lips together, looks up at the cloudless sky, and shakes his head. "And if I'd gone through with it, that would have been the worst mistake of my life. New Mexico changed my life."

I wait for him to tell me more, still in his arms, and study the small lines at the corners of his eyes. There are a few gray hairs at his temples too. Since he mentioned eight to nine years, numbers start rolling through my brain. "You left California eight years ago?"

"Nine," he corrects.

"Geez. I was only in my second year of undergrad and still on the medical track Mom and Dad insisted on." I hadn't realized he would be that much older than me. Five years, sure, but eight plus however long it was before he left California. Tucking my lips between my teeth, I look down for a second and meet his dark gaze again. "How old are you, Luca?"

"I was wondering how long it would be before you asked that question." His brows furrow, and he smiles a little ruefully.

"It's not that it matters," I rush to say. "I'm just curious."

Luca releases me then, and I feel a chill at not having our bodies pressed together. But he slides his hand down my arm and laces our fingers together. "We have to finish up breakfast and get on the trail," he says with a sigh. "Otherwise, we're not going to make it to the right spot to meet Emma for the night. I'll pack Lucy up and ride with you on Jasper, and we'll have all day to talk as we ride. Seems like we're gonna need it."

As we return hand-in-hand to the others in the group, my team members collectively lower their eyes to where our hands are joined. A flush of heat creeps up my throat and sets my cheeks on fire. I tuck my hair behind one ear and nearly drop Luca's hand. Then, I decide their opinion doesn't matter, and raise my chin proudly.

Eddie walks over, hands me a plate of pancakes, and winks. "*Well, heavens to Betsy,* look at the lovebirds!"

AFTER BREAKFAST, WE FINISH PACKING up the tents and supplies and head out for the final full day of the ride. This time, riding on the same horse as Luca is different. I no longer feel like a fish out of water on Jasper. In fact, riding him or simply being near him gives me more comfort than I would have imagined a week ago. Geez. I mentally shake that off because I don't want to consider the implications that I've fallen for someone in such a short period. But this thing between Luca and me has me feeling a lot of clichés at the same time—twisted in knots, feeling all warm and fuzzy, and off-kilter. Though, if I'm being honest with myself, I am a little smitten with the man who's currently wrapped around me.

He navigates Jasper with ease around our side of the herd, calling commands to Frankie on occasion when a few of the cows begin to veer off in one direction or another. But nothing like a couple of days ago when he was thrown from Lucy.

A couple of hours into the ride, Eddie and Calvin ride ahead of us, and Luca slows Jasper to distance us from the others. He clears his throat and then we both start at the same time

"Jack?"

"Luca?"

We share an awkward giggle and then I say, "Go ahead."

"I wasn't sure if yesterday meant anything to you." Luca squints off into the distance. "Until you accused me of all that this morning."

He's got a point.

"I don't think I was sure of it either," I say.

"I shouldn't have done it. You'll go back to California tomorrow and that'll be it. Even if we try to make things work, long distance relationships are always ill-fated."

However, he doesn't complain when I snuggle into him, so I enjoy the soft rocking of Jasper's gait and Luca's warmth surrounding me while I contemplate his words. It would be a challenge to be wrapped up in a relationship with someone a thousand miles away, but we could visit each other, right?

Luca stays silent at my back, allowing me to think things through, something other dates in the past have never done. It always seemed as if they needed to fill the void with useless words. Luca is different. Silence between us is okay, and I like that. I enjoy it so much I hold on to it for a long time and allow my mind to drift and examine my "love life."

The times I'd kissed guys in college or the few Tinder dates I went on after graduating, everything seemed unnatural—to the point that I started to wonder if I should try dating a woman. I thought about it for weeks and even considered talking to Mari about it. After all, she'd always been open about being bi-sexual and went on dates with both men and women on the regular. I just assumed I was straight and always tried with men. But after a year or so of worrying about it, I decided to focus on my career first and assumed when I met the right person it would feel natural, regardless of gender.

And here I am with Luca, feeling natural. The notion of him being the right person scares me because both he and Emma have mentioned how unhappy he was in California. How can I expect him to engage in a relationship with someone whose entire life is there?

I decide it's time to change the subject and look up over my shoulder at him. I wonder for a split second if he's contemplating the same things as me, perhaps not the failed attempts at connecting with anyone but his own failed relationship. "Tell me about Sonja," I say.

A frown crosses his lips, but he gives a small nod. "I said before that we met in college. Once we both graduated, we moved in together. It seemed like the expectation and the next steps. I landed the job at Google, and we were well on our way to a white picket fence with 2.5 children. She even got a cat within the first year of our cohabitation."

I wrinkle my nose.

"Yeah, I'm not a cat fan either. Anyway, she worked in marketing at several techie startups, bouncing between jobs regularly, and my career progressed until I received a promotion to director of research and development. At our celebration dinner, the hints at marriage started. A few weeks later, she was laid off from her latest gig and she stopped trying as much at her career."

"So . . . you believe all she wanted was to be a wife."

"The thought crossed my mind, but then she landed a job with a larger company. I popped the question the day she started, thinking the future was looking up." There's something sad in the way he says it.

"But?" I ask.

"We were already drifting apart. I think it was a last-ditch effort at the proverbial "us." But the engagement didn't change things. I worked longer and longer hours and didn't mind the separation a bit."

"Sounds familiar," I say. It's a connection with his state then, but I don't know that I've been distracting myself from other problems like it seems he was.

Luca continues. "Sonja started making extravagant wedding plans, and the disconnect between our goals led to many fights."

I smile. "You don't seem like the extravagant wedding type of person."

"I'm not. I would have eloped and been perfectly happy with the situation."

Interesting. It's a notion I can't dispute. I may love some of the finer things in life—designer shoes, Athleta yoga pants, having my hair done every four to five weeks, massages, and the list goes on. However, eloping sounds far more romantic than a big expensive wedding.

He takes a deep breath. "Plus, over the years, my health had gone really downhill. I went in for a regular checkup with the doctor and found out I was prediabetic. At thirty."

I give a small gasp and cover my mouth. He doesn't appear to be in poor health at all. Quite the opposite, in fact, with the way his torso tapers to his waist. I run a hand over his muscular thigh. "You apparently made some good changes," I say, half-jokingly.

He nods. "I went back to the office and called Wyatt, and the next morning, I was on a plane to Albuquerque." He laughs, then, as if he's dismissing whatever losses he might have had in that experience. "It's really a boring story, right?"

It might be nothing special to the average person—a story of lives diverging in a natural way—but I'm fascinated by it and curious. "Do you think it would have been different if she'd been as interested in her career as you?"

His body goes rigid behind me, and he answers, "Doubtful." But he leaves it at that.

The silence is back, punctuated by hoofbeats and an occasional moo from the cows.

I run a fingernail over the stitchwork on the saddle. "The kiss did mean something to me, Luca," I admit. "It's the first one I've ever had where I wanted more."

Luca

NIGHT FOUR HAS ALWAYS BEEN my favorite of these retreats. Relationships have normally been formed, or with the retreat goers, strengthened. Each time, a group shows up as strangers, but by night four, I often feel like I've made friends for life. I've always been aware that these new friends of mine would go back to where they came from, but I often get mail, texts, and updates, and I love having friends all over the country who remember their time at Thoroughbred Ranch as transformational.

This retreat is different. LivFit has been a good group. Most of them are the sporty types, some golfers, easy people to read and connect with. Bruce is a bit grumpy, but as long as he has his flask in the evenings, he's hunky dory and loose-lipped. But I won't miss any of them when they leave tomorrow. No, it's Jack I can't imagine parting with. Our eyes meet across the flames of the fire. I wish she was on my log. Instead, Bruce took a seat next to me, and she's too far away, sharing a log with Eddie.

"Whiskey's never tasted so good," Bruce slurs, swigs from his canteen, then wipes his mouth with a sleeve. "The only thing missing from this fire is a camp song," he adds.

My eyes meet Jack's again, and everyone laughs. If it weren't for the liquor, Bruce seems like the least likely candidate of anyone here to make such a suggestion.

"Hello Muddah. Hello Faddah," Bruce belts out.

Geoffrey of all people is the first to join in. Followed by Sean and then Eddie. Before I know it, even I'm singing along with this group of misfits.

When the song is over, Bruce declares between his bout with hiccups, "You guys are the best friends I've ever had."

"Okay, buddy," Geoffrey says, coming to a stand. "I think it's time for me to put you to bed."

"But da—" Bruce stops himself before he calls his boss dad. "Things were just getting good.

The fire flickers in a gust of wind. Eddie stands, looking into the blast. "*Well, it's a blowin' up a storm, so ya'll better hit the sack.*"

I snicker at his horrible southern drawl, and Jack groans at first, but then she chuckles too.

"Just a little desert wind," I say.

But really, he's having a blast, and it shows. So, we let him have his fun. He'll be talking about the retreat for ages, I'm sure. Others stand and start making their way to their tents.

"Can I help put the fire out?" Eddie asks.

"No, no," I say, too eagerly. "I'm going to sit out here for a bit and clean up so our morning runs smoothly. You get off to bed. It's late."

No one protests as one after another clumsily meanders over and disappears into their tents. Jack stays sitting on the other side of the fire, and we both stare at it until the flames get lower and the fire is nothing but glowing silt.

I take the water jug beside me and pour some on the fire. Smoke clouds go up to the sky. The moon is just a sliver this evening, and I can barely see Jack. She walks to me, and I put my hands on her shoulders.

"I guess this is goodnight," I say.

Jack takes my hand in hers, kisses my palm and then

my cheek and leaves my skin tingling where her lips touched.

Yes. Night four has always been my favorite.

Chapter Twelve

Jack

ORNING. THE MORNING OF MY last day in New Mexico came far too soon, and I'm even more torn today than I was yesterday. This time with Luca has been amazing. Tender and caring. I can still imagine his fingers trailing up my arm and the sweetness of his kisses. And after the real conversation we had on the ride yesterday, I feel more connected to Luca than it seems possible. This week has been so much more than I ever could have imagined. Or hoped.

The last thing I want to do today is go home, but there's not much choice. Last night, Emma mentioned that they had another group coming in on Monday, and I have a big project to get back to. Our pre-launch campaign is only two weeks away, and I have to bring the project to completion, at the very least.

When we met Emma at camp last night, she'd brought the wagon back. This morning, we unpacked

Lucy's load, and instead of riding with me on Jasper, Luca mounted up on her.

Now, I reach down and run my fingers through the cinnamon-colored mane, marveling at how silky yet sturdy the hairs are. Jasper is Luca's horse. Luca has tended to him at every stop, and there's something that's different about the horse when Luca is here too. It's as if he's settled . . . at peace, if that makes any kind of sense. "I miss him too, boy," I whisper to Jasper, and the statement takes me off guard.

Jasper points his nose in Luca and Lucy's direction and lets out a whinny that causes Luca to glance over. We exchange small, shy smiles, but I hold Jasper's reins steady to keep us separate by some distance. I may be imagining things, but it seems like even the horse is urging me toward Luca.

"It's okay, Jasper," I whisper. "If he's anything like me, he needs a little time to think during the morning's drive."

Jasper nickers.

"Do you want to be near Lucy?" I ask, starting to think she's the reason he's acting out of sorts.

The horse shakes his head. I blink several times, not believing what I'm certain is happening at the moment. Jasper pauses and, once again, actually shakes his head back and forth like he's answering my question.

I sigh. "Okay. Perhaps it is time for me to head home. I'm starting to hallucinate."

Jasper snorts. This time, I'm certain it's a sarcastic sound. I know nothing about horse communication, but it feels like he's giving off a ton of human emotions at the moment. And he hasn't been this vocal for the entire trip. It's too coincidental. I pet him, trying to calm him down. "Shhh"—I rub him down the long cord of muscles on his neck—"shhh. . . ."

"Hey, Jack!" Eddie rides up beside me and tips his cowboy hat toward something in the distance. "Looks like *the cows are about to come home.*"

I groan. "Sure does, Eddie, but I'm not sure that's the correct usage of that phrase."

He looks me up and down as we canter along. "Girl," he finally says, but this time it's with the normal Eddie sass I'm accustomed to. "You seem pretty low. Not what I would have expected after your ride with the hunk of a cowboy yesterday. And you two were the last awake around the fire, if I do recall." He wags his brows.

I try to smile over at him, but it probably doesn't come off with any kind of happiness.

He returns it with a smirk and one brow raised. We ride in silence for several more horse paces and then he lets out a long groaning-sigh, if that's even possible, followed by, "Guess it's girlfriend time. Dish," he says.

Rolling my lips between my teeth, I hang my head. My personal feelings and utter confusion aren't things I want to get all chatty about with a colleague. What if it comes back to bite me in the rump? I've listened to so many women motivational speakers who've advised against showing emotion with any professional acquaintances. Maybe that's a problem. Perhaps those women were only lucky in their careers. If there's one thing that's become abundantly clear on this trip, it's that

I need to welcome a little trust into my life.

"Give me a sec, Eddie. 'Kay?"

He lets the semi-silence simmer for a few minutes, and in that time, I'm not sure I have one coherent thought. Where I normally have a dialogue running through my brain, all I have in those few minutes are images flashing through my mental movie screen.

Luca sniggering when I fell down the steps.

The quiet conversation with Emma around the fire.

Snuggling into Luca while riding Jasper.

Eddie coughs, pulling me from my own internal Hallmark film, and he starts in again in his imitation drawl, "Wanna know what *I reckon*? If you *had your druthers*, you wouldn't be boarding that plane back to San Fran today."

"Is that so?" My voice is wispy, and I stare ahead at Gilbert Trading Post we're encroaching on at a pace that feels inch-by-inch, but also like a free fall on a roller coaster. I take a deep breath and steel myself. "You know what, Eddie, no. It's time to go home. I've got a product to launch in a few weeks that's been my dream for a couple of years now. I've lived it. Breathed it. It's my baby, and this . . ." I wave my hand around in the air. "All this is just . . . a distraction," I finish as Emma comes riding over.

I give her a curious look but then remember that Bruce offered to drive the wagon this morning, citing his hip was feeling it after so many days. I, for one, wasn't so sure he had sobered up completely from last night.

"Hey y'all!" Emma's voice is as chirpy as always.

I wave.

Eddie glances at her and back at me. "Hey, Emma. Maybe you can talk some sense into this one, because it seems *the porch light's on, but there ain't no one home.*"

As he rides away, I furrow my brows, because that one makes absolutely no sense. I think he just said I'm crazy, but that's nonsense. I'm getting back in my right mind for the first time in a few days. This was fun, but I need to focus on my goals and remember what I want out of life.

Jasper groans, almost as if he's put out with my thought process, but he's wrong. I have a full life back home.

Emma runs her horse in a circle and comes up alongside us, slowing to a canter, and watches as Eddie catches up to Calvin ahead of us. Luca rode over a few minutes ago to check in with Wyatt and I catch him returning as I glance over at Emma.

She asks, "How's the week been for you, Jack?"

"Good," I answer on autopilot. "I think I actually disconnected from work." I bite my lip, adding to myself, *perhaps a little too much.*

"That's honestly what we like to hear at the end of retreats. Some of the others have said the same thing. Fresh air does wonders for the soul, and most people go back to the office refreshed and with a new outlook on the job."

Hoofbeats announce Luca's arrival, and a dust

cloud billows up around us as he slows Lucy until we're cantering along in a line of three, plus Frankie, who trots along on the other side of Luca.

"Almost there," Luca says and looks off to the west, where there's a dark thunderhead gathering. "And just in time, it seems."

"It'll be a quick passing storm," says Emma. "We should be able to get the team loaded into the airport van before the rain comes, and we'll wait it out inside."

They're winding down on the trip and talking about the weather as if I'm not right here between them, so I stay quiet. But the incoming storm feels like a nail in a coffin, pounded in by some thunder god's hammer.

Luca continues, "I'd like to get the horses trailered up before, if possible. We're making good enough time that it should be possible." He looks across me, only making the briefest of eye-contact. "Can you let all the riders know to meet me to the right of the post ASAP? Wyatt will take care of the trade, and I'll load up."

"Of course," Emma says. "Although, Jack?"

I glance over. "Yeah?"

"With the rush to get onto the trail, I totally spaced calling the transport company to have them pick up the rest of your things from the ranch house. But don't worry; we'll ship it to your address in San Francisco first thing on Monday morning." She reaches over and squeezes my forearm. "I've gotta say, this trip has been one in a million. Really. If I don't see you, I hope you stay in touch. Maybe come back for another retreat someday."

Emma smiles at Luca, gathers the reins, and kicks

her horse into a gallop. She only slows when she reaches Eddie and Calvin up ahead. She points and gives her instruction and turns back. Meanwhile, Luca and I ride along for a minute, watching the storm roll in as Emma goes back to speak with the other riders on the LivFit team.

While I sit there, my hands start to shake and my heart begins racing. I'm working up the words to say my goodbyes, but they just don't want to squeeze past the knot in my throat.

"Ya know," Luca begins before I can find my voice. He reaches for me and takes my hand in his, and I trail my eyes from our connected hands up to his sincere, dark brown eyes. He seems a little nervous when he continues. "You could . . . ah . . . change your flight. Ride back to the ranch with me in the truck. Wyatt and Emma have to wrap up the business here and will meet us back there late this evening. I'll make sure you get to the airport first thing in the morning, so you'll only miss an hour or two of work."

I stop breathing. Yeah, that's exactly what I want. Maybe I need one more night with Luca. When I finally take another breath, a smile pulls at the corners of my mouth. Something warm fills my chest. He wants me to stay; wants a little more time. Against all the "go home" talk I'd been giving myself, I say, "I'd like that."

Luca

JACK'S HAIR WHIPS IN THE wind as the warm air, scented with the coming storm, comes in through the open windows of my truck. I fold up the middle console, grab onto Jack's left leg, and pull her closer. I want her sitting right next to me. She rests her palm on my upper thigh, and I'm convinced that this woman doesn't belong in Corporate America. No, I'm certain this is the exact place I should be and that she's always been destined to ride at my side in this truck. She fits so perfectly in the crook of my arm, like a key in the right lock.

The lights of San Francisco. The breeze off the ocean. The sounds of traffic and horns. All of it seems like a lifetime ago to me, but I wonder if I can convince her that the desert air is so much better for the soul. All I see is the expanse of New Mexico's rolling hills and the smell of vanilla that come off of Jack. Thunder rolls.

"Can you hold the wheel?"

When she wraps her small fingers around the leather steering wheel, I release my grip and roll up the windows until there's only a slight breeze coming through the cracks. I'm convinced that this is where I'm—no, *we*—are supposed to be. However, we also don't want to get drenched in the downpour.

She reaches for the radio. There's not many tunes out here except country music, so after a few button presses, "Cruise" by Florida Georgia Line comes on. It sounds a lot like a theme song. I wish the storm would stay away so we could keep the windows down and the wind blowing around us, but the first few droplets of rain splat into the windshield.

"Turn it up," I say and sing along.

We get close to the ranch as the song fades—the drive back is much shorter than driving cattle across the countryside—and I lean over to kiss Jack's cheek. "Are you okay if we take a slight detour?"

Jack smiles, and instead of pulling into Wyatt and Emma's ranch house, I drive down the road to the next dirt drive about a mile away. I squeeze the wheel tighter, anxious about showing her my baby, but the contractors have just finished framing and putting on the boards for the roof, and I want to share what will one day be my home with her. Her eyes widen as we pull up to where the driveway will circle in front of the huge porch. We both hop out of the truck and run through the rain to the shelter of the porch. Jack practically jogs inside the construction site.

"Luca," she says, looking at me. "This place is going to be huge. Look at these views!" She glances around at the hills off in the distance

. I take her from room to room, explaining my vision for each. Then, I show her my bedroom with the massive en suite bathroom. I point to where a soaking tub will be with views of the hills through the large window.

I find myself trying to sell this place to her. Because for some reason, I crave her approval. I want to know that Jack could see herself here. Even though, realistically, I'm not certain that that could actually happen. She'd be walking away from a whole life in California. I grew up in the city. I've worked with the corporate types, and working here, I've also met enough city slickers on these retreats to know I'm the exception to the rule. The normal city-folk stay in the city and come here when they want a break from the proverbial rat race. Many talk about moving away, slowing down, but so few ever do.

As she walks through the place, pointing out what

she can see from the studs alone, I want those touches that are uniquely her in this place too. I suddenly can't imagine ever bringing another woman here. Shoving my hands into my pockets, I shake that thought out of my head.

"It's so big for one person," Jack says as we return to the truck.

I start the ignition, but before driving away, I turn to her. "I do hope I'm not alone forever, Jack."

Her entire face distorts, and she averts her eyes. "No, no. Of course not. And you won't be. I mean. I can't believe you don't already have women lined up for you. You're so great, Luca."

"You don't have to say that, Jack," I say and mean it. I didn't bring her here with any kind of plans, but I can't help the thoughts of her. Of us living here and working with Wyatt and Emma, and the horses… all of it. I put the truck into drive and pull around the driveway, eager to get the horses unloaded and in their stables.

"But I mean it," she says quietly, her smile fading into something else. "Someday, some woman will be lucky enough to have you love her, and this house will be filled with kids. And if I ever come back here for another corporate retreat, there will be little Lucas running around."

Jack looks out the window, and we ride in silence until we get to Wyatt and Emma's.

I unload the horses and we systematically and silently lead them into the stables and to individual stalls. Jack hangs out with Jasper, brushing his coat and sprinkling kisses all over him. Lucky horse.

She lets out a big sigh. "I'm going to miss you so much, Jasper," Jack says, and he snorts.

Jasper leans into her, prodding her to give him more rubs. She happily obliges with a little laugh, and it's clear they've formed a strong connection too. I can sense in him that he doesn't want her to leave either.

"Will you miss him more than me?" I ask. My voices drips with so much desperation that it's almost embarrassing. But alone with her, I feel vulnerable. If I knew how she felt or that this whole thing was definitely only a fling to her, perhaps the thought of bringing Jack to the airport in the morning and saying goodbye to her wouldn't be ripping me apart inside.

"I don't know," Jack says, smirking in my direction. "Jasper is pretty cute."

As usual, Jack steers the conversation in another direction, and I know that if we're going to have a real conversation about what we are, I'm going to have to just go for it.

Soon.

Jack

I DONNED A JOKING FACE and made a quip about Jasper, but it was a show. I can't believe I'm thinking this, but no, I will not miss Jasper more than I'll miss Luca. However, telling him how much I want more time with him scares the living daylights out of me. In the last few days, I've forgotten all about work and the project. Do I really care? Does the thought of letting someone else run my project bother me? Will the world stop if I don't go back and finish it on time, make a million sales, and get a promotion? Will I be so much worse off if I don't prove that a girl can perform just as well as all the men around her? Somehow, I think the surprising answer to all these questions is *no*.

The home Luca is building is going to be beautiful with tons of space for kids and dogs to run and play and better views than I would have imagined possible in New Mexico. I always imagined this state would look like the armpit of the earth—flat, dusty, no plants, and too hot for animals to come out during the day.

I was so very wrong. It has lots of brown but there's green too. The trees aren't redwoods with tall canopies, but they're lush around the desert floor. The mountains in the distance are simply majestic. I could get accustomed to looking out over them as the sun sets for the day.

I gulp in a breath and blink several times to clear my thoughts. I can't reconcile my life so far with the notion of staying here, yet. . . making a life with Luca seems, not only possible, but nice. Adventurous. Peaceful. But I can't let whatever's here in the desert air cloud my senses this way. No. I need to go home and at least finish the work I've begun.

Jasper's snout is warm against my lips as I give him a final kiss goodbye and turn to Luca. He tilts his head toward the door. "Ready to clean up for dinner?"

Just the word sounds delightful. Trail baths and wet wipes can only do for so long. I have dry hair, so I don't wash it daily, but after the trek through the desert, my scalp is even beginning to itch.

Side by side, we meander back toward the ranch house. The storm has passed just in time for us to see the sunset set the desert on fire with the last red rays of the day.

"You know," says Luca, "after the pandemic, I don't think you'd have to give up your career to live here."

My head whips around to look at him. "What?" I'm not certain, but I think he might have just asked me to move to New Mexico. We've been growing closer, but I was certain he'd let me go home tomorrow and we'd perhaps talk for a while before we move on from this little interlude in both our lives.

He shrugs and squints into the setting sun behind me. "I hear that many companies are letting their employees work remotely now. I read somewhere that they're even downsizing office space and creating something called 'hotel desks' for when people absolutely need to be in the office."

I tuck my lips between my teeth. The thing is, he's not wrong. I've been splitting time between my condo and the office at a seventy-percent remote rate.

Luca climbs the steps to the front door of the ranch house. The funny thing is, the ranch house looks nothing like the place we left a few days ago. That's probably me, but it seems so much more welcoming now. Homey.

But this isn't my home. It's Wyatt's, Emma's, and Luca's. My home is a modern condo overlooking the bay in San Francisco. I'm going back tomorrow, and that's all there is to it. I follow Luca up the few wooden steps to the landing and lean back onto the wooden post at the top.

"Luca," I say.

He turns around, half-smiling, and I hate myself for what I have to say. I despise myself so much at the moment that I don't think I *can* say it.

He places one hand above my head on the post and wraps his arm around my waist. The contact feels so good I lean into it, into him.

Luca lowers his head until our noses touch. "Yes?"

With him this close, enveloping all my senses, all thoughts leave me. The only thing that comes out of my mouth is a whispered, "Thank you" before he crashes his lips to mine.

It's a demanding kiss at first and then it softens. His hand moves into the back of my hair as he deepens the kiss, and I let out a small moan. There are so many unsaid things . . . an ocean of the unknown, the unexplored, and the possible in the dance of our lips and tongues. My hands find his face, and the rough stubble scrapes on my palms. The hand at my back pulls my body flush with his, and I give him everything I have in that kiss. Before long, my eyes start to prickle and burn. I pull away before my tears betray me.

Luca

NO ONE WHO HAS EVER met me would call me a romantic, not even my ex, Sonja. Pragmatic? Sure, I get that one a lot. But my entire body tingles where her lips were just touching mine. I walk to the office, where all the keys are lined back up. The entire house is put back in order after LivFit left. Well, after most of the LivFit employees left.

I tuck my hands in my pockets and look at all the keys, nicely hanging in their places, each one with a unique key chain. I don't want to be presumptuous, so I grab every key and walk out to where Jack still stands on the front porch. She's running her fingers over her lips, and I wonder if our kisses affect her the same way they do me. I won't ask, though, because I have to let her go tomorrow.

"Looks like you have your pick for a room tonight," I say, holding out my hands full of keys.

She looks at me and then studies the assortment. I hold my breath when she starts digging through them. Her teeth sink into her bottom lip, and she tilts her head back and forth as she takes an eternity to read each single digit. It's making me insane, but I hold utterly still. That is, until she holds up the key chain for room number five. My room.

"My pick," she says, dangling the keys in front of me. Her lips are forced into a straight, serious line, but her eyes smile up at me.

Relief washes over me. I wanted her to choose my room, to stay with me, but I worried she wouldn't want to. She is so much younger than me, after all, and so focused on that career of hers. Although, I am not going to be one to argue.

"Good choice," I say, setting the rest of the keys down on the porch railing, something Emma can have a fit at me over tomorrow. I take Jack's hand in mine and lead her upstairs to my room.

When I walk in, I'm surprised at how much my room smells like her from when she slept in here the day before we went on the cattle drive. It looks the same, but the vibe feels different.

"Now that I know you a little better," Jack says, staring at the framed pictures on the far mall, "This entire room makes so much more sense."

Both were taken by me. The one on the left is a photo I took standing atop twin peaks in San Francisco, and it's a view of the city with the water in the background. The photo next to it is of the open field on day one of my very first cattle drive here at Thoroughgood Ranch. The same field, in fact, where Jasper almost gave Jack a heart attack. Both pictures are such opposites, but both also represent a huge part of my life.

"I wanted to show the contrast." I stand next to Jack and study the pictures together.

Chapter Thirteen

Jack

MOMENTS BEFORE THE SUN CRESTS over the mountains, I stand in the kitchen, sipping my coffee and waiting for Luca to come downstairs to take me to the airport. The rooster starts in again like it did the first morning I woke up in this bed here at Thoroughgood Ranch—in Luca's room. At that time, my mind and heart weren't at odds with one another like they are this morning.

I close my eyes and recall images of him on the trail, the way he saved me when Jasper bolted and how he constantly read into my hopes and the fronts I put on for LivFit. I only imagine the feel of his skin against my palm and the way his stubble would scratch the tips of my fingers. The first time I met him, when he fumbled his way into this room while I was changing, he was clean-shaven. I couldn't deny how appealing his sharp features were then. But when I saw him last, he had a ruggedly handsome, movie-star look after a week of not shaving. I never thought that was possible in real life. I only imagined it was the work of talented makeup artists.

He kissed me lightly last night before we parted, and how sweet it was, but it was also a goodbye. I'm more convinced of that this morning. I've only known this man for a week, so I can't sacrifice myself and everything I've worked toward for a title of Mrs. Or even CEO of House Luca.

I need to go home. While I'm here, I keep having these flashes of Luca and me, scenes we've already experienced together as well as imagined scenes of us in his finished home. I can clearly see a future of Luca chasing me around the kitchen island and sweeping me into his arms or us sitting together on the front porch in cute little rocking chairs while the sun sets over the mountains. Or us taking a long trek with Jasper down one of the dusty trails. It's not fair that I had to travel more than a thousand miles to wake these feelings inside myself.

Last Tuesday morning seems like another lifetime, and the memories of my arrival seem like something I watched in a movie. But that person was me. *Is* me. I have to slide back into that Jack's skin and resume my life. It shouldn't be too hard once I'm back in California, especially since I'm at peace with going home.

The kitchen door swooshes open, and Luca walks inside with a wide smile. "Top of the morning, Jack."

I swallow the last of my coffee, smile, and go to the coffee pot for a refill. As I'm passing between him and the island, Luca touches my forearm. I turn, with my eyes downcast and fighting the prickling sensation happening in my sinuses.

I inhale sharply, attempting to shake off the awkwardness I'm feeling, and smile up at the first man to make me think of a real relationship. He's so intuitive and sensitive and—no, I have to stop thinking about these things.

I wiggle the empty cup between us. "It's going to be a long day." Then I turn around.

As soon as I take a step in the direction of the coffee, the door crashes open, and I smack straight into another man's chest, bouncing backward.

I blink a couple of times at Wyatt, who's shifting his eyes back and forth between Luca over my shoulder and me. He holds my elbows to steady me, and I wriggle free, reaching up to swipe the hair out of my face. Geez, I'm starting to think it's this house that makes me so darned klutzy.

"Ah…um…Jack?" Surprise and then understanding light his eyes, and he scowls at Luca. "How unexpected, meeting you here."

Luca

"WYATT," I SAY, READING MY best friend's accusatory expression. I wasn't ready to share this with him yet. I wanted it to just be between Jack and I for a little while longer. "Have you heard of knocking?"

Wyatt furrows his brows and tilts his head. "It *is* my

kitchen"

I grumble between clenched teeth, as if my reasons should be obvious.

Jack fidgets and rushes toward the coffee pot.

Wyatt chuckles again. "I need a little help reshoeing Pirate, but that can wait. I'll leave you two alone."

He goes to leave but pokes his head back in through the door first. "And guys," he says, looking at both of us, "Emma and I literally called this on day one. So, you're welcome." His laugh reverberates through the kitchen before he closes the door behind him.

I join Jack on the other side of the island and brush her hair away from her face, breathing her in. "This week has been—" I begin to say, but before I have a chance, Jack interrupts me.

"It was fine," she says, waving me off, avoiding eye contact, as she finishes pouring the coffee.

Fine? The connection we have feels so much more than fine. It is incredible. Perfect. It was the most in tune with another person I've ever felt. If Jack's assessment of our time together was that it was simply fine, then what does that mean for every other woman I've dated?

"Are you okay?" I ask, sliding my hand down to her elbow and urging her to look at me.

She strains to meet my gaze, so I pick her up and set her on the counter.

"Yeah, why?" Jack asks, face devoid of anything that would be helpful in reading her.

"It's just that—" I stop myself, completely stuck in my

head. There's so much I want to say, but I'm scared to put myself out there. But if I don't, I'll regret leaving things unspoken between us.

"Your stay with us wasn't just fine for me," I say. "Getting to know you has been incredible. I was in a long-term relationship, Jack, and I'm here, telling you honestly that I've never felt the way I feel about you for anyone."

Jack's body stiffens, and she pulls her lips into a long line on her face. When I take her hand in mine, she goes limp.

"Luca," she says, "I'm not good at this stuff." She rolls her lips between her teeth, a gesture I've come to understand is her version of the word 'um.' It's absolutely adorable. Her shoulders rise as she takes a deep breath and continues. "It's not that this wasn't great. It was. More than I ever would have imagined. But if we treat it like there's a hope for a lasting relationship with a thousand miles between us, it'll make today harder. I'm leaving. I have to leave. You're staying." She runs her hands down the center of my chest. "That's our reality."

My brain sticks on the great part, and hope surges forward. I step away and then pace back and forth before coming back to Jack.

I cradle her face in my hands. "It doesn't have to be our reality. You could stay and work on the ranch. You're a natural. You could find a job in town or work remotely for LivFit. Whatever makes you happy."

Jack runs her hands through her hair. "Stay?" Her voice shoots up an octave. "Here, with you?"

"Yes, with me," I quickly respond.

"Luca," she says. "You're amazing. This place is great. But

I've only known you for a week, and I have a job back home. A lucrative job with a future and advancement opportunities. A real career path that I've worked so hard to develop. There are so many reasons why it's utterly unrealistic for you to ask me this."

My stomach feels like I've been punched. We stare into each other's eyes, and I haven't told her the most important part . . . the fact that I think I'm in love with her. This feeling is so much stronger than what I had before. Even if a week ago, I would have insisted love grows more slowly than this. But this week has proven me wrong. As unlikely as it seems, I've fallen hard for Jack. I can see forever with her, but based on the goodbye in her eyes, I'm certain my sentiments will only scare her away. She doesn't seem in a position to accept my love.

"Should Emma drive me to the airport?" Jack asks, running a finger around the rim of her mug.

"No, no," I say. "I promised you a ride today, and I'll give you one."

"I'm sorry, Luca," she says, but I'm not sure what she's apologizing for.

"It's fine. It's fine," I say, but in truth, I don't know if I'll ever feel fine again.

Jack

THE TRUCK STARTS UP WITH a roar and in the next second a female voice wails over the radio, "Cowboy Take Me Away." In a single move, Luca drops the truck into drive and presses off button on the car stereo.

Guilt gathers in my gut as I lean an elbow on the door next to the window and prop my chin up to stare outside. In the distance, I see the stable. Wyatt is outside with his mostly white stallion. Jasper is outside too, standing off to the side, swishing his tail and munching on hay. A lump forms in my throat, and I think about asking Luca to turn right toward the barn. When I look over, though, he's scowling, so I decide not to press my luck.

I turn back to the window and mouth, "bye Jasper," and then wipe away a tear that leaks from the corner of my eye.

Further in the distance, Luca's future home grabs my attention. Another possibility I'm saying goodbye to before I even open the door. But I did open the door, and that's the problem. I can hear my mother now. *Jacqueline, why don't you think these things through?*

It's okay, though. I've built my life in San Francisco, and this is just a blip on my radar. Transient. Everyone has passing interests. Mari certainly does, although right now, I wonder how she manages to stay so disconnected.

I hug my bag to my chest for the whole ride, as if it's a life jacket on a sinking ship called the *SS Jack*. There's no conversation, no laughing, no singing, and no cuddling like there was on the ride back to the ranch house from the trading post. The cab of the truck simply feels empty today. The rumbling diesel engine and the groaning the wheels make as we hit a few bumps along the way are the only sounds to punctuate the painfully silent ride.

Probably a mile after we turn onto the pavement toward Albuquerque, my phone starts buzzing. Messages from coworkers, surely. I ignore it, not wanting to face work until well away from Luca. For some reason, that would feel like pouring salt into a gaping wound.

Luca drives and I sulk.

And the hour seems to last a lifetime.

Luca

THE SIGN AT THE DROP off area reminds me that no parking is allowed, and that this area is strictly meant for quick drop offs only. As if I needed the reminder that I'm dropping Jack off and may never see her again. I turn the engine off but don't remove my hands from the steering wheel, nor do I look over when she opens the door to the truck and gets out.

I suck in all the air I can, before I get out, and grab her bag from the back. She stands in front of me, and I hold her bag hostage. If I don't hand it over, she can't go back to California. My logic is awful, but who says love and logic belong in the same sentence?

Jack surprises me when she pulls me toward her. Her delicate hand caresses the base of my neck and she stands on her tiptoes and draws me down until our lips meet. It's less of a kiss, and more breathing the same air as the other person, as if it's necessary for us both to survive.

She releases me, but then wraps her arms around my waist and buries her head in my chest. "I'll never forget this week, Luca. For as long as I live."

I kiss the top of her head. All the words I want to say are clogged in my throat.

"I won't either," I say instead of what I feel. A tear

escapes my eye, and I wipe it away before Jack can see.

Jack pulls away from me one last time, and I hand her bag over, fighting a smile over how gaudy the thing is and the memory of it splayed out on my bed. We never discussed keeping in touch. We haven't even exchanged numbers. What's the point? I don't want a text from her telling me that she's arrived safely. It will only make me miss her more.

"Take care of Jasper for me," Jack says. "And maybe bring me up from time to time. So he doesn't forget me."

I chuckle through the heartbreak. Because sitting around and talking about Jack when she's so far away seems inevitably painful.

"Alright, City Slicker," I say, trying to keep things light between us because, if I don't, I'm going to fall apart. That much can wait until the ride home. I playfully punch her shoulder. "You have a flight to catch."

"Bye, Luca." Jack turns and walks through the airport doors. She never looks back.

Chapter Fourteen

A week later

Jack

My Nespresso machine broke this morning, so I'm a bit cranky as I stroll up to the double glass doors with the LivFit logo etched across them. One of my peers, Anthony, arrives at the same moment as me and reaches for the door handle with a huge smile. He's so proud of himself for helping a little lady through the door, and I have to remind myself of what the workplace harassment training video I watched earlier this week told me. Opening the door for someone is a common courtesy, not a sexist slight.

I know this, and if I had enough caffeine pumping through my veins, I might have been a little happier to step through before him. Instead, I unclench my jaw and put on a smile. "Thanks, Anthony. Haven't seen you since we got back. How's R&D program going for the implantables?"

Anthony has a background in the medical device field, so he was brought on to lead what would hopefully break LivFit into that market. From my understanding though, devices that are going into someone's body require a whole lot more rigor to meet government standards. My jaw hit the floor when I first saw that his project plan would run for seven years in order to gain all the regulatory approvals.

"It's going well enough. We just hired a fantastic lead engineer, and I'm really excited about her ideas."

"Her?"

"You bet. I worked with her at a prior engagement, and she's probably the smartest and most strategic engineer I've ever met. I was thrilled when she accepted my offer to come here. After all, we don't develop life or death devices."

I give him a genuine smile then, finding myself pleasantly surprised by his high praise. "That's awesome, Anthony," I say as we enter the elevator. "I'd love to meet her."

"She's making the rounds with the team this week, but we could arrange lunch early next week."

I agree, and we ride the rest of the way up in silence. As we're leaving, I start toward my office on the left. Anthony hangs a right. "Have a great day, Jack."

I nod, my mouth already watering for a coffee. Thank goodness I bought a second Nespresso machine for my office. I pull out my mobile phone and scroll through emails, rounding the corner when I reach the end of the hall, and I come up short when I see two people standing in front of my office door.

I stop dead in my tracks and gasp.

The woman is Jane, the head of Quality Assurance on my team. She's young and curvy and has the cutest blonde curls to match her huge blue eyes, which at the moment, are wide with delight. She has her left hand splayed out in front of her with her eyes wide, staring at a ring on a very important finger. The other person is my curmudgeonly, flask-drinking, hip-aching peer, Bruce, and he's holding the tips of her fingers and staring at the rock.

It's a good thing I'm not holding a cup of coffee, because I surely would have lost my grip and splattered it all over Jane's delicate pink trapeze dress and pristine white Keds. She's always had that sweet look about her as if she was stepping off the movie screen out of one of those '50s beach movies.

Speaking of movies, someone put reality on slow motion as they both look over at me and grin happily. Innocently.

I furrow my brow as I study them. What about Jane's fiancé? They were the perfect Ken-and-Barbie couple with this huge wedding planned up in Napa next spring. Jane had been showing me different dress options for months. I always had them pegged for the married with 2.5 kids couple by thirty. Why would she consider Bruce?

And oh, what a midlife crisis Bruce must be having. I sure hope it wasn't the New Mexico air that changed his mind. What about his wife Margaret?

There's a bump on my shoulder, and I'm caught so off guard that I sway sideways into the wall.

"Your prototype is the talk of the office, Jack," Eddie says.

Jane skips over to me. "Just look at it, Jack." She thrusts her hand forward, and the diamond catches the fluorescent lights above, making it glint.

Bruce limps toward us too, wearing a small congratulatory smile.

Jane continues. "All the tests came back clean from our QA team this morning, so we're a go."

I compose myself as the pieces click into place. "That's . . . um . . . wonderful." I blink and smile. "Let me see."

"It's *'um . . . wonderful'*?" Eddie mimics my stuttering reaction with his eyes narrowed. "You didn't—" He tucks one arm under the other elbow and points back and forth between me and where Jane and Bruce had been standing and gawking over the ring.

I wave a hand in the air, a feeble attempt to wave off the misunderstanding. "No. Of course not. That would be ridiculous!"

Eddie raises his brows and purses his lips.

The next minute is the most uncomfortable business moment I've ever experienced, and I keep my eyes on the ring for much longer than necessary. There's no way I'm giving voice to what I thought was truly happening between Bruce and Jane. Geez, I do need a strong shot of coffee.

Finally, Bruce breaks the butter-like silence. "I hear you have an editor from *The Knot* coming out this afternoon for an interview. Congratulations, Jack. I was quite doubtful that fitness and jewelry would mesh so well, but you've proven me wrong. I'm excited to see where this takes the company." He claps me on the shoulder and hobbles down the hall toward his office.

Jane returns to her desk.

Eddie holds out a hand in the direction of my still-dark office. "I think we have a meeting."

I tuck my hair behind an ear and open my office door. I had totally forgotten that Michelle Francis from *The Knot* was going to be here just after lunch with a full photography crew. So, I'm going to have to do some kind of magic to get myself together before a PR meeting. When I enter the office, the lights come on automatically, and I head directly for the table by the window where I keep my coffee maker, dropping my laptop bag on the desk in passing.

The door clicks shut behind me, followed by a creak of my guest chair as Eddie plants himself on the opposite side of my desk. I rustle through the top drawer, where I keep the Nespresso pods, searching for something strong. When all I find is decaf and French vanilla, I drop my head back and groan.

"That bad?" Eddie asks.

"Apparently," I say and turn to him. "What were we even meeting about this morning?"

"You asked me to prep you for the interview this afternoon. Remember?" He looks me over with one brow raised, sits forward, and opens his laptop. "However, it seems . . ." Eddie makes a few clicks, types something, and closes the lid. "It seems you're going to need more than the hour we had scheduled."

He pushes the laptop away, stands, and holds out his hand. "Let's run down to Cuppa Joe's and get you a triple espresso, then we'll see about fixing you up to camera-ready Jack."

I breathe deeply. "Deal."

Outside the LivFit doors, I loop my arm through Eddie's. We walk like that for a block and a half before he says, "You know, Jack, you're not the same at all since we've returned."

"Really?" I furrow my brows. "How so?"

"I think you know, but don't want to admit it."

He can't be talking about Luca. No, I decide. "I have no clue what you're talking about. I just need coffee like I need air to breathe."

We swing into Cuppa Joe's. Eddie waves to the barista and holds up two fingers. When his partner, who is currently attending Berkley and working here, nods at us, Eddie blows him a kiss.

I nudge my coworker playfully. "Must be nice to be the number one customer."

"It has its . . . perks."

I groan.

"Be right back, hon."

Eddie slips away to grab our coffees, and I scan

through my emails while I wait. When he returns and shoves the paper cup in my hand, I sip then let out a satisfied "aahhh."

"Come on, you have an appointment."

I look at him askance.

"Girl, you look like you could have slept in those slacks. There's a pencil skirt, white button down, and fresh hair style waiting for you at my salon around the corner."

Every bone in my body sighs with relief. "Oh my gawd, Eddie, you're a lifesaver!"

He checks his watch. "Get a move on, doll, or we'll miss the appointment."

Outside, he stretches out our stride to the end of the block and we whip around the corner. I plow straight into a brick-wall of a man. The half-cup of coffee crushes and splatters between us, and he crouches to where the cup falls. I gasp and hold my hands out, in shock and saddened over the loss of my espresso, but then I look down at the man. He's wearing boots and a cowboy hat, and for an instant, my heart starts fluttering like a herd of butterflies. But it plummets when he stands up and hands me the remains of my cup, and I realize it's not who I thought. Yet even his drawled, "I'm terribly sorry, ma'am," makes me yearn for a man that I decided to run from only a week before.

Eddie pulls some napkins from his pocket and hands them to the cowboy. "She's on her way to change, so this is the best I can offer you."

He accepts the napkins and dabs his dark blue shirt

and jeans. "It's all right. At least I'm wearing a dark shirt." He tips his hat, says, "Ya'll have a better rest of the day," and walks on by.

My lungs expand, and I take a long-awaited breath.

"Yup," says Eddie, "*sad is the house where the hen crows and the rooster is silent!*"

"Aargh, I thought you were done with that?"

"Well, doll, I've got one more for ya." He hands me his coffee and we press on toward the salon. "This career you've cooked up *ain't gonna amount to a hill of beans* if you don't have someone to share it with."

Luca

JASPER LEADS ME ON THE trail. The morning sun rises up over the hills in the distance. I haven't taken Jasper out, just the two of us, in too long. When we reach an open field, Jasper doesn't even gallop. Instead, he looks back at me, and puts his head down.

"I know, buddy," I say. "I miss her too. But today we'll have a new group arrive, and you'll have someone new to ride you."

My words are void of truth. And Jasper knows it. I miss everything about Jack. The way she puts her hands on her hips when she demands attention. The way she bites her bottom lip before she's going to share something vulnerable. The way she stared into my eyes when I shared something. Like she understood and cared about what I was saying.

I also miss getting to protect her when she was scared,

even though I knew she never needed my protecting. Jack is the most self-sufficient person I've ever met, and I have no doubt that someday I'll be reading about her in some business magazine, and I can tell everyone that I knew her once.

When I arrive back at the ranch, the van with the new group is pulling down the long driveway. Wyatt and Emma wave me over, and I get off of Jasper and hold his reins as we wait. This is always the exciting part. The group gets out of the van and is a mixture of both men and women. Then, I see a petite brunette, hair down past her chin, and I grow excited.

Her eyes shoot in my direction, and a smile extends across her face, but my stomach drops. It's not Jack. Of course it isn't. She made her need for her career a top priority. As much as I hope, we just aren't written in the stars.

Late that night, I am in bed, head resting on my arms, when there's a knock at the door.

"Hey," Wyatt says and pokes his head in the door. "I hope I'm not disturbing you." He takes a seat near my corner table.

I sit up in bed. "Not at all. What's going on?"

Wyatt looks at me, concern all over his face. "You're not yourself, Luca. Are you okay?

If you can't say it to your best friend, who can you say it to?"

"I have no clue what Jack did to me in such a short period of time, but I'm in love with her, Wyatt."

He nods like I said the most obvious thing in the world.

"Did you tell her?" he asks.

"Well, no," I respond. "I didn't want to scare her."

"So, instead, you let her go?" Wyatt stands up and leans back against the table.

"I didn't let her do anything. Jack chose to leave. I asked her to stay. Her life is there. Mine is here. End of story."

Wyatt takes a deep breath and holds it. He always does this before he's going to say something important. "Emma and I love having you here. We know your new home is nearly complete. But all of that stuff can be figured out. Home is wherever you make it, Luca, and whoever you choose to make it with."

"I've made my home here. For good reason."

Wyatt shrugs and stands up straight. "To be in love with someone who doesn't know you feel that way, well," he walks to the door and pauses, "that sounds like pure torture to me."

I stare at the door for a long time after he leaves, thinking about his words and why he'd come all the way to my room to tell me such things. Then I groan and flop over on the empty bed.

Sounds like torture—ha! It *feels* like torture to me.

Jack

Driving is always a strange feeling to me, but I do

own a car. It normally remains parked and charging in the underground garage at my condo building, but today, it's a necessity for the hour and a half drive south. I need someone to objectively ground me. Eddie was too close to the situation, and Mari is definitely the fly-by-the-seat-of-her-pants kinda friend. So, this is a first and strange, even to me, that I'm turning to Mom and Dad for advice.

But here I go.

Before backing out of the parking spot, I connect my phone to the car stereo system and search through the streaming app. I'm in a mood, so my fingers hesitate over the keys before I give in and type "country" into the search bar. Another first.

Before, that was the only station that would tune in near the trading post and Thoroughgood, but this is a choice. Knowing nothing about the music genre, I select the first station that appears.

As I pull onto Highway 101, the list is on the third song, and I'm a bit curious why all of them so far comes with mixed-up warm and fuzzy feelings. Are there any country songs about something other than love?

About the time I make it to Palo Alto on my way to San Jose, a duet comes on, and I tap along on the steering wheel. About halfway through the song, I'm getting choked up, because every word seems to narrate the way I felt about Luca. It talks about choices and them not wanting to live without the other. There's one line that keeps repeating, so it must be the title: "Nobody but you."

When it starts talking about going down separate roads, I reach over and punch the power button. I can't. I . . . just . . . can't. Different roads are the right answer.

Right?

Mom and Dad will set me straight. They have always been the most practical voices in my life. They tried desperately to steer me back toward the medical path, which would likely have been an easier road to success for a woman. I wouldn't listen then, but today, I need their logic and reason to reassure me I made the right decision.

I exit 101 onto the south loop around San Jose, deep in the heart of Silicon Valley now. And I can't handle the silence anymore, so I turn the radio back on and flip through my playlists on the screen until I find my girl power play list. A little P!NK, some Lizzo, and Beyonce. Turning it up, I sing along and feel immediately more like myself.

Pretty soon, I turn south and pass the hospital complex where both my parents have worked ever since I can remember. This whole area is familiar, down to the turn I took every day for four years before I left this snooty, rich-kid area and went to Berkley. There was money there too, but I found a great group of girlfriends there, and those years defined me.

I suck in a long breath and sigh. Memory lane at its finest.

After driving onward toward The Willows for another twenty minutes, I pull into the driveway of my parents' mansion, the home they built in the woodsy hills between San Jose and Santa Cruz just before my 13th birthday. It's positioned among a couple of vineyards and a Buddhist getaway, so a bit away from the pretentious neighborhoods where most of my high-school peers lived.

Still, the place is a monstrosity, making Thoroughgood Ranch house, with five guest bedrooms, a huge foyer, office area, and dining room for twenty people, seem small.

I cut the engine, silencing Alicia Keys's "Girl on Fire," and stare at the double front doors for a long minute.

Do it, Jack.

As I open the door, my mother steps outside and skips down the steps with her arms wide open. She's shorter than me by about six inches, and she wears her dark hair pulled back in a knot at the base of her neck. Looking into her face is almost like viewing myself in a mirror. She still looks young for her age, thanks in part to her Latina heritage. But her beauty routine helps too. The perks of being in the medical community in one of the richest areas of California and having a best friend who's a dermatologist, I suppose. People have often said we could be sisters. Along with her genes, Mom also imparted her secrets to me, so I'm hopeful I'll still have her youthful look in another twenty-five years.

"Nena," my mom says as she squeezes me tightly.

"Hi, Mom." I hug her in return.

"It's been too long, *mija*," she says.

As she drags me up the steps and inside, I have the urge to apologize, but hold it in. It seems too cliché to say I'm sorry.

The smell in the house, as usual, draws us toward the kitchen. To answer my mother as we walk, I offer, "I'll try to get back more often once this project wraps up at work." I'm not sure it's the truth, but hopefully it'll keep the lectures away. As a doctor, she knows the story of being busy with work. For as long as I can recall, she went into work at strangest hours, leaving me with—

"Nana," I say as I spot my grandma at the counter cutting peppers.

Mom leaves my side as I scurry around the counter to give Nana a big hug and then I peek in the pot she has boiling.

"Tamales?" I ask.

Nana smiles broadly and says in Spanish, "When Sylvia told me you were coming home, I made sure we had the ingredients." She understands English, but refuses to speak it, kind of like me with Spanish. I only speak it when absolutely necessary, even though I grew up speaking both. And being bilingual has also opened a number of doors for me.

I concede with greeting my grandmother though. "*Te Quiero, Nana. Gracias.*" I drop a kiss on her cheek.

"Jackie, welcome home." Dad enters the kitchen with his arm around my mother.

I cringe and object, "Dad, please." Then, I notice how cute my parents are together and my heart melts. Married for nearly thirty years and still touching, holding each other, and showing affection when they move. As if they revolve around one another.

Dad raises one hand in surrender, not letting go of Mom. "I know. It's Jack or Jacqueline," he says, rolling his eyes. "Come here, then, and give me a hug, *Jacqueline*. I refuse to call my only little girl by a boy's name."

"What about Jackie Chan?" I tease as I circle around the island and give him the requested embrace.

It feels good to be here with them. Family. Strangely enough, it reminds me of another home more than a thousand miles away. Even stranger, it makes me wonder how the home that's currently under construction will turn out.

Nana chases us out of the kitchen with a shooing motion. "The first batch will be ready in an hour. Go. Relax." .

Mom and Dad head for the living room, and I follow. They sit on the love seat, and I take the perpendicular armchair. There's lemonade in a pitcher on the table with four glasses. Mom pours three. Dad takes one. She hands one to me and reaches for the third. "What brings you down?"

I roll my lips between my teeth and stare at the mint leaf garnishing the drink.

"What your mother means," Dad begins, "is we're delighted to see you, but it was quite a surprise when you called yesterday to say you were coming."

Mom smiles and lays a hand on Dad's knee. "Sorry, I forget my bedside manner with family."

My eyes follow her movement with some strange feeling pulling in my chest. "It's okay," I say. "I do have something I want to talk about." Then, I quickly bury my face in the glass.

My parents exchange a look, and my dad says, "We're always here for whatever you need, Jacqueline. You know that, right?"

The sweet-sour drink cools my throat, and I let out a sigh. "I do."

Something lights in my mother's eyes. "Is this . . ." Her eyes roam between me and Dad. "Is this about a . . ."

"Man?" I offer, and she nods. I suck in another deep breath. "Yeah. It is."

"Well, where is he? Why didn't you bring him?" she asks, and I can feel her excitement growing.

Mom married my dad when she was twenty-six, still in med school, and she gave birth to me the same year she graduated. I have no idea how she managed school, residency, and having a baby all at the same time. Perhaps it was having Nana here to help her along the way.

She's never mentioned it to me directly, but since I finished my MBA, I've felt her desire for me to find someone almost every time she looks at me. Perhaps that's part of the reason why I stayed away so much.

"Mom—" I blow out a long breath. "He's not here, because he doesn't live in California. He lives in New Mexico."

Dad blinks at me, confusion clear in his scowling brows.

"Yeah, I know. And no, he didn't come here."

"What were you doing in New Mexico?" Mom asks.

"Well, you see, I planned this work retreat." I shake my head and guzzle the rest of my lemonade. Then, I tell them the whole story, leaving out the intimate times, of course.

As I talk, my mother leans toward me and hangs on

every word. And my father, always the cooler, calmer, and more collected one, sits back with a small smile pulling at one corner of his mouth.

"So," I say, coming to the whole reason I came to speak with them. I need their practicality. "I need you both to tell me I'm too rash, too spontaneous, that I'm rushing in to something that'll ruin my life. Explain to me why I'll be giving up everything I've worked for if I decide to try this thing and . . . maybe move out there." I sink my teeth into my bottom lip and stare at them expectantly.

Mom turns to look at my dad, who pulls her closer and kisses her on the forehead. And then she settles into his side and faces me again.

Dad begins, "Jacqueline, all those things you want us to say would be blatant lies, and I don't think that's what you really want to hear."

My jaw drops. "But you've always pushed me so hard. In school. When I switched degree paths, you were so disappointed."

"*Mija*," my mom adds, "all we have ever wanted was for you to be happy. We worried about you entering a corporate world. It just didn't seem to fit your personality. I'm so sorry it seemed like we disapproved. Think about it, *mi princesa*. Does your job at LivFit really make you happy?"

"Of course it does," I snap.

Dad holds up one finger. "I mean truly happy. Does it incite the energy and excitement you felt when you just told us about Luca and Jasper? Do your eyes get all glassy and dazed when you talk about your work meetings like they just did when you told us that story?"

I open my mouth to object again, but nothing emerges.

Because Dad's right. A grin spreads on my mom's face and she clasps her hands under her chin as realization washes through me. No, career won't ever give me the warmth I felt with Luca. No, prestige is overrated. Apparently, Luca realized that a long time ago when he moved away from California. I want that kind of peace and steadiness I found in him. I'll finish out this program and then hand things off. Once that book in my life is closed, Geoffrey Tanner and all of LivFit can take their misogynistic crowd and incessant meetings and stick 'em where the proverbial sun doesn't shine.

Chapter Fifteen

Luca

I DIG THROUGH OUR ARCHIVED FORMS in the office until I find the stack that says LivFit. I'm aware that I'm violating every privacy rule we have in place, but I have to find Jack's address. It must be on the form she filled out.

"Let me help," Emma says, entering the office. I don't even need to explain what I'm doing. She already seems to know.

"Here," Emma says, handing me a form. I look at it, and there it is, right in front of me. Jack's address. I know the address well. I lived in a building on the next block. How did Jack and I never run into each other? Or did we at one point? But we were both too absorbed in our own lives to look up for a moment and notice each other.

Wyatt pops into the office. "Should we go with a one-way ticket, or round trip?"

"She may not feel the same way," I say. "Is this stupid?

Am I insane?"

"No!" They both yell at the same time.

"Let's do one-way for now," Emma says. "And you're not being stupid. You'll never know how she feels unless you tell her."

"And you're really willing to live back in the city?" Wyatt asks.

"I'd live anywhere for Jack."

"Pack your bags," Wyatt says. "We'll take you to the airport in the morning."

Jack

MY FRIEND, MARI, SITS ON my bed. She's still in pajamas from our sleepover, her hair is in a messy blonde bun at the top of her head, and she sips on a freshly brewed cappuccino from my brand-new Nespresso machine. She has her MacBook in her lap and is browsing through the gallery pictures on the Thoroughgood Ranch website.

"I can't believe you didn't take one selfie with this guy you're going to go back to see." She drops her hand beside her with a huff. "None of these pictures have a good view of him."

But I already knew that. "I'll send you a photo as soon as I get there, but . . ." I think for a second to recall the actor's name. When it comes to me, I ask, "Do you remember that actor Giulio Berruti from that romance trilogy we binge-watched a couple of years ago?"

She looks up with her blue eyes huge and her mouth gaping. "Gabriel's Inferno?"

"Yeah," I say absently, reaching for the stack of new jeans I ordered. "He looks a lot like him, except for with dark-chocolate eyes."

Mari closes her computer, finishes her coffee, and then flops backward onto the messy bed. "I wish I could go with you to meet him. It sounds sooo… romantic."

Chuckling, I continue sorting through my clothes and packing. "Do you want some of these skirts?" I ask. I'll keep a couple, but I don't think I'll have the occasion to wear them much in New Mexico. It's nice that Mari and I are the same size.

"Sure," she says. "But I really don't want you to go. What am I going to do without you?"

"You'll be fine, and it's not like we're never going to see each other again. I'll be back at least once a month for my job at LivFit."

Mari sits up as I'm zipping up the suitcase. "I'm still shocked they agreed to let you work from another state."

Quite frankly, I am too. "They didn't have a choice if they wanted me to stay on. I think Gina from HR pressed the issue because of the diversity factor. Plus, I'll be traveling for a while to publicize the LivFit in Luxury products." The photo shoot and interview with Michelle Francis from *The Knot* went spectacular and launched a stream of interviews, including two in New York next month. One with *Good Morning America* and another with the *Today Show*.

After the launch, I'm remaining on the LivFit staff

as the product owner and visionary for the product line. However, we agreed that I won't be taking on new products, only working to keep the luxury line relevant to the market. I'll be stepping away from the director-level position so I won't have any more direct staff management accountabilities. Eddie will be taking over for me, and I'll report to him, which is a-okay by me.

All this will give me additional time to get settled in New Mexico . . . assuming that's still what Luca wants. We'll see after I surprise him at the ranch later today. If I've planned things correctly, they should be in between groups.

I check my phone for the time. My flight leaves in three hours. "Shoot! I need to finish up and make my way to the airport. Can you get me a cab?" I ask Mari.

"Argh. I wish I had time to take you before my first meeting." She picks up her phone and types a few things. "Should be here in forty minutes."

Perfect.

Luca

People rush around me at the airport, and a woman running bumps into my arm, causing my bag to drop to my feet. She doesn't even bother to turn back, as she rushes off in the opposite direction. I sigh and pick it up, and as I'm standing up, I catch sight of a billboard sign on the wall. It's the cover of a magazine, entitled *The Knot*, and pictured there is a set of enlarged wedding bands with a woman in a black pencil skirt and white shirt standing in the background. A woman I'd recognize anywhere. The headline reads, "LivFit Director Jack Moreno brings luxury to fitness wearables."

Smiling, I turn toward the exit and another guy bumps into my backpack. I shake my head and press onward. It's been a while since I've been around this many people. The last time I saw my parents, they visited me on the ranch. I used to be one of these people. Rushing to catch my flight. Work brief case in tow. Button down shirt nicely ironed and tucked into the latest fashion of men's dress pants.

And here I am again. Willing to put myself back into this world. For love. Maybe I am romantic after all. A child stares at me as I walk by. I look so out of place here. My plaid shirt, tucked into my jeans, and cowboy boots that I rarely leave home without. I can't imagine putting back on a pair of Cole Haans. Even if I get back into Corporate America, I'm finding a way to keep my Ropers as a staple to my wardrobe.

Jack. I think back to the day she arrived on the ranch. So unsure of herself as she looked around. At the time, I thought it was arrogance she was displaying. In hindsight, she felt as out of place in New Mexico as I do in San Francisco. We were meant for two different worlds, it seems. I start to doubt myself as I follow the stream of people and the signs for baggage claim.

What would life look like here? I could get back into the tech industry, although I'd have to start near the bottom again. I'd leave for work in the dark morning hours and return home in the dark too. But it all will be worth it if, when I open up the door at the end of the day, Jack is there. We'll sit around and tell each other about our days, compare notes. Order Chinese takeout, and sit on the couch, her feet on my lap as I rubbed them.

Home is where you make it. That's what Wyatt said, and I believe him. Almost as much as I believe Jack and I have a real chance at happiness.

What if she doesn't want that life though? Or doesn't want that life with me?

The bags circle through, until I see mine appear. I grab it, and head outside. It's a cool, foggy day, and my years of living here all come flooding back to me. It wasn't all bad, right? The food, culture, and ability to make a lot of money. The friends. Maybe I'll have to reach out to a few of my old friends eventually. The weekend brunches and boat rides in the bay. There were so many good times spent here. When the ranch comes into my mind, I shudder that thought away. Jack is worth leaving it all behind.

Cabs line up, but people beat me to them. I wait for almost all the ones there to move along and for another one to appear. This time, I step in front of a man that tries to get in front of me. *See, it's all coming back,* I tell myself. The vehicle comes to a stop, and I wait a split second before reaching for the door.

As I grasp the handle, the door flies open, first hitting my knee. I stumble a little and then, yep, I can't breathe for a moment. San Francisco. Everyone is in a hurry, and common decency sometimes goes out the window.

"Excuse me—" I begin to say with a strain, and then a female exits, face hidden to me.

"Can you kindly get out of my way?" she says, but there is nothing kind in her voice at all.

Her voice. Hairs stand up on my arms with the familiarity. I know that voice, and it's music to my ears. She turns around and grabs for her rolling bag, and I put my hand around her arm as she sets it on the curb. Then, her gaze meets mine.

"Jack?" I ask.

"Luca?" Her eyes widen and flash with hope, at least that's how it seems.

The man who was waiting beside me takes his opportunity to jump into the cab. As it takes off, I pull Jack further away from traffic.

"What are you doing here?" I ask, taking in the sight of her. She's beautiful. Sunglasses on top of her head, a light coat and jeans. Ankle boots. And the biggest, brownest eyes I've ever seen.

"Me?" She laughs. "What are you doing here?"

"Well, there's this girl that lives here. In San Francisco. And there are a few things that I wanted to tell her."

Jack's face distorts, as if she's concluding I'm going back to Sonja. She reaches up with one hand and slowly moves her sunglasses from her head to cover her eyes.

"Jack." I chuckle. How could she believe otherwise? "*You're* the girl."

Jack

LUCA'S HERE.

Luca. Is. Here. In San Francisco. And he just said—

No way! "You came here for me?"

He chuckles again. "Yeah, I did," he says, and his smile is brighter than the morning sun in a clear-blue New Mexico sky, and I read so many emotions across his face. Then, his brow furrows. "But you must be, um, going on a business trip." His entire posture falls.

My eyes prickle and happy tears fall. "No." I grin. "No. I was on my way to New Mexico."

His arms come tentatively to my sides, and there's a question forming on his lips.

I dip my chin, tucking my hair behind one ear with one hand and removing my glasses with the other. I can't have a barrier between us anymore. "You see, Luca, there's this guy that lives there."

He drops his backpack on the ground and draws me closer to him. His hands rest on the small of my back.

I let my shoulder bag slide down to join his pack at our feet, and slide my hands up his arms until they reach the back of his neck. "And he has this amazing horse."

"Go on," he says, arms tightening around me.

Some random couple walks by. The guy whistles and the girl says, "Kiss her already."

I ignore them, because I'm lost in this amazing man in my arms. "And the two of them, this man and horse . . ."

Luca presses his forehead to mine, and I'm so close now I can feel his heart pounding in his chest.

"Well . . ." I shrug. "They kept something of mine when I came back to California a couple of weeks ago."

He tilts his head, eyes narrowing. "I didn't find any—"

I put two fingers across his lips; mine are almost to his now. "My heart, Luca. They kept my heart."

Fireworks flash in Luca's dark eyes, and he crashes his lips to mine.

Epilogue

Three months later

Luca

WHEN I PICTURED MY RANCH home finished, this is pretty much exactly my version. A mixture masculinity infused with feminine touches. Jack's décor surprises me. It's not too girly, but instead, simple elegance. There are candles that smell like her on the fireplace mantle. An aged picture of kids holding hands and standing around a tree in our den—a replica of her favorite photo from her nana's childhood album, Jack told me when she hung it between the two photos that defined the two big parts of my life. Now, the trio is complete. San Francisco Bay, the view of the desert, and Jack's family in between.

This is our home.

Jack comes barreling into the house, clapping her hands. When she sees me, she runs and launches herself into my arms, wrapping her feet around me. I can't help but love this woman. Her zest for life is contagious.

"I take it the closing went well," I say.

"Yes. After all that drama and back-and-forth, the paperwork on my San Francisco condo is signed and sealed, and the money will be wired tomorrow."

I take Jack's cheeks in my hands and kiss her. Sometimes I feel the need pinch myself, wake myself up from this imagined blissful life. But it's no dream. Not a figment of my imagination, and with the blessed months we've had together, I'll hopefully get to do this for the rest of our lives.

"This is cause for celebration," I say.

Jack hops out of my arms and walks into the kitchen.

"I agree. I'm thinking we go grab Jasper and Lucy and have a picnic down by the pond." She starts pulling things out of the refrigerator, and I go to the fridge and pull out a bottle of sparkling cider.

"Well, my rich girlfriend . . ." We walk hand in hand to the stables and my other hand carries the full basket. "What will you do with all of this money?"

Jack looks up at me. "I want to help pay for this house. I mean, I feel so guilty that I live here for free."

"Nonsense," I say quickly. "I won't have you giving me a cent of your money."

"Well," Jack continues. "Invest it. Or, put it toward the ranch."

"Kids college fund," I say, and Jack stares up at me and smiles. I love that talking about our future doesn't scare her. I'm older. I've lived more life, but we're on the same page about what we want.

"Or that." She smiles brightly at me and nods. "Yeah. Or that."

Jack

We enter the stable, and Luca takes the picnic basket from my arm, strolling over to the far side of Jasper's stall. He sets the basket on the stack of hay bales along with the two champagne flutes and bottle of sparkling cider. Since he freed up my hands, I stop and open Lucy's stall first. Luca takes Jasper from his stall and starts toward where I'm waiting for him near the saddles with Lucy's reins in my hands.

He wears a sly smile, petting Jasper's muzzle as they approach. Then, suddenly, they stop a few paces from us. Luca taps Jasper just above his front leg and clicks a few times in the back of his mouth.

I'm amazed as Jasper lifts one leg and backs up until he's in a bowing position with one knee on the ground and his other front leg forward. The horse lets out a whinny and Luca sinks to one knee too with a hand reaching into his back pocket.

My eyes widen and I cover my mouth while I stand there with both my men on a single knee before me.

"Jacqueline Ana Moreno," Luca says.

"Yes!" I squeal.

Luca chuckles. "I haven't finished."

"Oh. Sorry." I roll my lips between my teeth and try

to wait.

Luca opens a little box, putting a huge marquis diamond on display. I look closer and read the logo I had created: *LivFit in Luxury* embossed in golden lettering on the top inside of the ring box.

"Jacqueline Ana Moreno," Luca says, "I promise that I will do everything under the New Mexico sun to make your life the best it can possibly be. I will be here to support you through all life brings. I'm hoping you'll do the same and agree to honor me by becoming my partner for the rest of our lives."

I stay utterly quiet. Pools of tears form in my eyes, but I'm not sure if he's done.

His lips stretch, and he asks, "Will you marry me?"

Jasper snorts as if he wants in on the game.

I jump. And squeal again. And clap. Then, I pet Jasper on the nose as Luca releases him from the bow. I kneel in front of this man, who has become my entire reason for living, then I take his face in my hand and look into his eyes. I place a gentle kiss on his lips and then pull back. "Yes, Luca. Yes. I love you so much." I kiss him again and feel the relief sinking into his body as he returns the kiss.

After several moments, our kiss starting softly, deepening, then grows tender. Once more, I pull back and look at my fiancé. "You never had any reason to doubt. I want to be your partner in life more than I've ever wanted anything. I'm yours. A million times over. Always. Forever."

The End

Book reviews are the best way to support an author!

If you enjoyed this story, please leave a review anywhere you can give a shout out!

Also, if you enjoyed this story, check out other works by the authors:

Leah Omar:

https://bronzewoodbooks.com/leah-omar/

Susan Stradiotto

https://bronzewoodbooks.com/susan-stradiotto/

www.ingramcontent.com/pod-product-compliance
Lightning Source LLC
Chambersburg PA
CBHW061434210726
48287CB00007B/2203